Lethal
DISSECTION

DOBI CROSS

Luxhaven
Publishing

ISBN paperback, 978-1-958987-08-7

Interior & Cover Design by Luxhaven Publishing

Editing by JD Book Services

Proofreading by Lisa Lee Proofreading

To JC, Grandma D, and DC, whom I love more than life itself.

READ MORE BY DOBI CROSS

Dr. Zora Smyth Medical Thriller Series

Lethal Emergency (Prequel)

Lethal Dissection

Lethal Incision

Lethal Obsession

Lethal Reconciliation

Lethal Adhesion

Lethal Retraction

SEE ALL OF DOBI CROSS BOOKS

at https://dobicross.com

AUTHOR'S NOTE

Thank you for choosing LETHAL DISSECTION.
Zora Smyth is a character I was fortunate to meet a
couple of months ago as I brainstormed ideas for my
first medical thriller story for an anthology.

Zora was already a surgeon in the initial story, but I
always wondered what life would have been like for
her as a medical student. That's how LETHAL
DISSECTION was born. Writing LETHAL DISSEC-
TION has been a great walk down memory lane for
me as I relived my days as a medical student, though
nothing as fascinating as this happened at the time!

It was important for me as I penned this series to
have Zora Smyth not be some super hero or a person

with extraordinary abilities, but an everyday person who through the journey of the next few books comes to fully understand and appreciate who she truly is and is able to heal from the childhood baggage she's carried all her life.

Please continue this journey with me in LETHAL INCISION. You can grab your copy at https://dobi-cross.com.

Would you also want to be notified when the next Dobi Cross book releases? Sign up at https://dobi-cross.com.

Once again, thank you so much for purchasing LETHAL DISSECTION and for meeting Zora Smyth. If you enjoyed it, please consider leaving a review at your favorite retailer or recommending it to a friend.

Thanks again for your support!

Dobi Cross

Lethal
DISSECTION

She woke up, went to work, and died. No one told Martha Adams she'd go this way.

The evening was like any other. Martha exited her office building around eight-thirty p.m., clad in a light blue coat over a pinstripe grey A-line dress from her favorite clothing store. The early October air had turned chilly, and a gusty wind blew her strawberry blonde hair in all directions. Martha brushed her hair away from her long face and pulled her coat closer around her frame. She hated the cold.

She scurried along the cobbled sidewalk in her haste to get to the train station. The streets were deserted—the financial district, where she worked, basically shut down once the last throng of workers headed home around seven p.m. Martha hadn't planned to leave the office so late, but her boss had imposed a deadline on her work that night without prior notice. So she'd ended up cancelling her date with Tim in accounting, which had put her in a foul mood.

Tim had finally asked her out after she'd had a crush on him for the past six months. Martha had thought he'd never notice and was shocked when he'd finally approached her. She'd been looking forward to the date. Maybe she shouldn't be so vexed with her boss who'd always been nice to her and had approved her early promotion a year ago. But Martha had been hoping to score a kiss from Tim today. It'd been a while since she'd felt the arms of a man around her.

The *click-clack* sound of her heels on the sidewalk filled the air as she hurried down the street. The overhead lampposts flickered and then died, plunging the street into darkness.

Martha's heart dropped, and she shivered. Unlit streets gave her the creeps—she never liked to linger on them longer than necessary. So she wrapped her coat tighter around her frame and hastened her footsteps.

As she neared the subway station, the lights from

the station illuminated the jagged potholes on the road, and Martha watched her step as she crossed to the other side. Now only a dark alley stood between her and the subway on the next block.

Martha exhaled a sigh of relief and checked the time on her phone. She could make the next train if she hurried. Only twenty minutes more, and she'd be home with Mr. Snickers, her tabby and best friend in the world. If she knew him, he'd be scratching at the door by now, waiting for her return. Mr. Snickers tended to pee on the floor when he was anxious, but Martha hoped he'd used his litter instead.

As she tucked her phone back into her coat, someone bumped into her, and she lost her grip on her handbag.

Martha yelped and jumped back. She heard a muffled 'sorry' and turned to see a man in a hooded jacket scampering away. Her arm hurt where the man had brushed against her, and she rubbed the area. Martha was tempted to mouth off at him, but she held her tongue instead. It was more important she caught the train on time.

She hurried toward the station, but Martha noticed her gait slowing. Soon it became difficult to put one foot in front of the other, almost as if she'd been drugged.

Her heart quickened. What was happening to her? She'd been fine until a minute ago. Was she having a stroke? Martha had heard it could happen to young people too.

Then she remembered the man who'd bumped into her, and she touched her arm. Had he done something to her?

Soon Martha's arms grew limp, and her legs became too heavy. She crumbled on the floor, her head not hitting the pavement by some miracle. Her vision grew hazy, and she shook her head to clear the fog. She tried to speak, but her voice didn't work. *Someone help me!*

A shadow fell over her.

Martha looked up, expecting a good Samaritan. Instead, a hooded face came into view. Cold soulless eyes locked onto hers like magnets, and she flinched. It was like staring at death.

Martha's heartbeat thrashed in her ears. Her body trembled, and she screamed, but no sound came out. Only the distant noise from the subway train echoed in the air. She wanted to flee, but she was locked down on the pavement.

Trapped. Immobile. Helpless against what was about to happen to her.

Then her head fell back as her world dimmed, and then turned black.

Martha Adams opened her eyes to see a big wicked-looking cleaver knife hanging over her head.

She screamed, but now her cry was choked back by a piece of cloth stuffed into her mouth and held in place by wide strips of grey duct tape. Her strawberry blonde hair lay tangled behind her head and rubbed against her neck.

Martha shivered and looked down. She was completely naked. She tried to move her body, but there was no give. Her hands and feet were shackled by metallic cuffs to the steel table beneath her.

Her heart beat loudly against her chest, and she broke out in a cold sweat as her body trembled. She tried to fold into herself, but the restraints held her back.

Martha took quick harsh breaths to calm herself and squeezed her eyes shut in the hope that she would wake up from this nightmare. But when she opened her eyes a few moments later, she was still in the same room. A dark room that appeared to have been abandoned for some time.

Old metallic equipment lay at awkward angles along the left wall. The right side featured a large metal door that seemed so fortified she couldn't imagine an ant getting through. There was an old, musty, and nausea-inducing scent in the air that reminded her of the morgue she'd gone to when Great-Aunt Debra died.

She'd called it the room of death. Just like this one felt.

Panic rose in her throat, and she struggled against her shackles as the grey walls threatened to close in on her. Martha didn't care if they left marks on her body from the effort. The hooded man must have brought her here, and she had to escape from whatever he had planned for her. Even if it seemed impossible. It didn't help that the big cleaver knife hung too close to her face and looked like it might swing down at any time.

She heard the distant sounds of heavy footfalls headed in her direction. The footsteps grew louder and louder, and then stopped in front of the steel door.

Martha's pulse raced. She struggled again to free herself, yet the effort was futile. She looked around for a weapon but found none. Not that she would have been able to reach for it anyway. But she couldn't give up.

Her stomach twisted when she heard a key inserted into the door. Bile welled up in her throat, and she felt like vomiting. A squeezing pain seared through her chest, and her breath came out in short gasps as the key turned in the lock. Martha felt liquid dribbling down her legs, pooling between the folds of her buttocks resting flat on the table, and she turned her head away in shame.

The metal door creaked open, and a beam of light shone through the doorway. She shut her eyes as if willing it away. The door shut with a loud bang, and the light disappeared. The room was once more plunged into darkness.

Martha heard the footsteps moving toward her. Her pulse accelerated with each advance, and she shut her eyes tighter and balled her fists.

A thought pierced through her frantic mind. Maybe she could pretend she was unconscious and buy more time that way. Time that would give her a chance to escape. So she tried to even her breathing and relaxed her hands.

Soon the footsteps stopped beside her. The man said nothing, but Martha could hear his heavy breathing.

Then he leaned closer, his foul breath assaulting her senses. The hair on her skin stood, her body itching to flee, yet Martha kept as still as she could.

A rough hand grab her forearm. A second later, a needle pushed into her arm, and the painful jab made her yelp.

"Goodbye, Martha Adams. This is for Anna," she heard a gravelly voice say.

Her eyes flashed open to see a man in a black mask and hooded jacket. It was the devil again.

Martha screamed. No, she couldn't die! Terror raced through her bloodstream as she thrashed against her restraints. Her mind scrambled to unravel the mystery—who was this Anna? Martha couldn't remember.

Her pulse sped up, and suddenly, she couldn't get enough air. Her breathing grew rapid, and her lungs felt like they were being crushed under a weight. Martha jerked against the table, trying with every-thing within her to break free.

But the restraints of death refused to let her go.

Regret at everything she was about to lose flashed through her. Mr. Snickers, all alone. Tim. A missed chance at love.

As her limbs grew weaker and weaker, a tendril

of her mind finally wrapped itself around a memory —Anna.

But it was too late.

Her body lost its battle as Martha took her last breath.

2

---

ora Smyth arrived early in the morning at the Gross Anatomy lab of Lexinbridge School of Medicine. The lab was housed on the first floor of a colonial style red brick building that must have been built in the early seventies, but which had been renovated in recent times to accommodate the modern facility.

As a first-year medical student, Zora had explored the building the day before and had been pleased to find an adjacent technology-enabled classroom for medical instruction, dedicated changing areas, and locker rooms on the same floor. The upper floor of the building had been converted into offices for the professors and instructors, while the main equipment supply room and the janitor's closet were in the basement. Each floor had its own set of restrooms.

Zora pushed open the double doors of the white-walled lab. The faint pungent smell of formaldehyde mixed with a mossy earthen odor overpowered her nose and threatened to make her retch.

Tears stung her eyes, and she blinked thrice to clear them. She stopped for a moment and riffled through her scrubs pocket. Where was it? Zora was pretty sure she had stuffed it in there.

Aha! Found it! She held up the lemon-tinged handkerchief like a long-lost treasure. With no time to waste, she pressed it against her nose and took quick deep breaths to cleanse her lungs.

Zora's desire to empty her stomach contents eased. Too bad she couldn't hold the handkerchief to her nose all the time, so she took one final deep breath and tucked it back into her pocket. It was enough to keep her for a few minutes before needing another sniff. She would have to get used to the smell, but that wouldn't happen today.

Fifteen stainless-steel dissection tables were lined up before her in rows on either side of the room, and a body-shaped mound covered by an aqua-colored sheet rested on each one. Every table boasted its own computer screen and a ceiling-mounted surgical lamp that allowed each team to view images and text clearly.

The computers were all connected to a central terminal which the instructor could manipulate to either show the same image across all computers or release to allow each team to view images of their choice as they worked at their own pace. Large orange bio-hazard containers under each table would collect the body parts that were eventually separated from the cadavers. A second smaller hazardous waste container was available to collect disposables such as gloves.

Anatomical materials and equipment used frequently in the lab were stored in a separate facility accessible through a door on the far left. As she walked toward the back of the room, Zora could hear the low humming sound of the ventilation system that exchanged stagnant air for cool breeze.

She pulled out a set each of nitrile and latex gloves from her other scrub pocket as she reached her assigned table, donned the nitrile gloves first to keep the smell of the cadaver off her hands, and then the latex gloves that provided a better fit for the dexterity needed to dissect the body.

Each medical student and two team mates had been assigned a cadaver. For today's class, the professors had switched the lab to take place first from eight a.m. to ten a.m., followed by lectures in the adjacent classroom from ten a.m. to twelve noon. Zora's team had agreed she would make the initial cuts on the cadaver before they joined her at eight. It was seven-thirty a.m. now.

Her lab partners were squeamish at the thought of cutting into a human body. Zora didn't mind doing it for them; after all it'd been just as hard for her when she'd seen her first dead body. She'd helped a college friend—whose parents owned a local funeral home—in preparing a body for viewing and had become closely acquainted with the toilet bowl during that time. Her previous experience didn't take away the queasiness she felt now, but her chances of retching in the lab at the sight of a dead body were lessened—though not gone completely, from what she'd just discovered.

Zora needed to be good at dissection if she wanted her dream of becoming a surgeon to come true. She couldn't afford to miss any step in the process, and the odds were she might never get the chance again. Cadavers couldn't be found on the streets—each body had been donated as a precious contribution to science, and Zora didn't treat this gift lightly.

The professors had spent yesterday preparing them for their next nine months at the lab, showing them proper dissection techniques, and sharing the rules and regulations. Zora was both excited and nervous to start.

She pulled back the aqua sheet. A body lay prone on the table, its contours indicating it was female.

Zora let out a sigh of relief. She'd been afraid she'd have to turn the cadaver on her own if it wasn't in the right position. The thought of doing it with dead arms draped around her as she manipulated the body almost made her want to retch again.

She took small deep breaths to calm her stomach, then clasped her hands together in a moment of silence for the cadaver. Once she was done, she was ready to start the dissection process.

Zora walked around the body, observing it from all sides. There was something different about it, but she couldn't place what it was. The burning smell of formaldehyde assaulted her nose, and her eyes watered again. The smell seemed much stronger on the body than she'd expected. *Maybe that's how it usually is,* she convinced herself. She pulled out the lemon-infused handkerchief for a quick inhale before stuffing it back in her pocket.

The cadaver's skin had a greyish tinge, but there

were no obvious scars. The body looked young—there was no wrinkling of the skin or age spots and appeared well taken care of while alive.

But Zora noted that it appeared a little bloated. She dismissed it as probably leftover gas from the gut bacteria's breakdown of the body tissues. The cadaver's long blonde hair was swept off her back, and it looked shiny, something Zora would not have expected from a cadaver. *The luster should have been all gone by now,* she thought.

Zora grabbed her mini notebook from her lab coat and wrote down all her findings. She would ask one of the professors later about it.

Her notes complete, she dropped the notebook back into her coat and picked up a scalpel from the instruments tray at the body's feet. She hesitated for a moment but then drew a deep breath and made a horizontal cut from shoulder to shoulder. Zora followed it quickly with a vertical cut along the spine and another horizontal cut above the tailbone.

It soon became obvious that something was wrong. Blood oozed out from the cuts and flowed over the body and down into the recessed tabletop. Wasn't it supposed to be formalin?

The scalpel clattered from Zora's hand onto the table as understanding dawned. Blood as fluid like this was only found in a body that was either alive or had died recently. Not in a cadaver.

With her heart in her mouth, Zora took a step back, and then another, then turned and ran toward the doors. She pushed them open, sprinted toward the end of the hall, and raced up the staircase two steps at a time. She turned into another hallway at the top of the stairs and ran to the third door on the left. It was the office of the main professor taking them through the course.

Without bothering to knock, Zora jerked the door open and raced in.

A bespectacled set of eyes looked up at her with annoyance. It was obvious he'd been reading his morning paper before she'd interrupted.

Zora put her hands on her knees as she struggled to catch her breath. "Professor, you...need... to...come."

The round face, with owlish glasses and greyed temples, suddenly looked concerned. "What is it?"

Zora straightened as she continued to take quick breaths. "A body in the lab... Something's wrong," she said.

The professor sprang to his feet, sending his seat rocking to the side. He grabbed his lab coat from the coat rack at his far left and donned it as he took quick strides around his desk and headed to the door.

Zora turned and followed him, her hand holding the side of her waist. She struggled to keep up with him as he turned down the hall and raced down the stairs. Soon they reached the lab. He breezed through the doors, his eyes drawn to the uncovered body at the back of the room.

The professor marched to the table and saw the blood pooling onto the sides of the body. Zora caught up with him and watched as he grabbed a latex glove from his lab coat, donned it, and ran a finger at the back of the neck. He held up and examined the gloved finger which now had a powdery substance on it. The skin beneath the area he'd touched was no longer grey but creamy white. The professor moved his hand to the side of the neck and felt for the carotid pulse.

Zora peered closer. "What's wrong with this body?" she asked.

The professor didn't answer.

Instead, he dipped his other ungloved hand into his lab coat, brought out his cell phone, and called campus security.

3

I t was now mid-morning, and the lab had become a beehive of activity. The doors were blocked off by yellow tape with a policeman standing guard. Two detectives had arrived, one tall with lion mane hair and a heavyset jaw, dressed in a dark blue jacket that hung loosely on him. The other —clad in a black leather jacket that barely covered his rotund belly—was much shorter with thinning brown hair and a protruding forehead.

A petite lady in a grey suit strode in behind them with a big black case, a young man in blue jeans and green shirt trailing in after her with a camera strap slung around his neck. Zora guessed she was the medical examiner.

The detectives quickly homed in on Zora and the

professor and ushered them both toward the classroom next door.

As Zora exited the lab, she saw her classmates and a few other faces she didn't recognize milling around in the hallway, but none approached her.

The tall detective led them through the classroom door and toward the center of the room. The cushioned chairs, each with its own desk, were arranged in a lecture theatre seating style with a large central lectern. The detectives leaned against one of the desks closest to the lectern, while Zora and the professor slipped into nearby chairs.

The tall detective pulled out a pen and a little notebook from his jacket and addressed them. "I'm Detective Morris, and this is my partner Detective Shepherd. I'm assuming you made the nine-one-one call," he said, gesturing at the professor.

"I'm Professor Braun. Yes, I did after Ms. Zora Smyth brought the case to my notice."

Zora's eyebrows rose. She hadn't expected him to know her name.

"Can you remember what time she came to you?" Morris asked.

Professor Braun looked at Zora. "I believe it was seven-forty-five a.m." The detective made a note in his little book. "I had just finished reading the newspapers. It takes me about fifteen minutes every morning to do so, and I like to read it at seven-thirty a.m. before the chaos of the day begins," the professor continued. "She burst into my office and told me there was something wrong with a body in the lab, so I raced down. I saw the body lying prone on the table with first cuts on the back."

"First cuts?" Shepherd gave the professor a questioning look.

"We teach the students to make three initial cuts to start the dissection of any cadaver," Professor Braun expounded. "A horizontal cut from shoulder to shoulder, a vertical cut along the spine, and a third above the tailbone. I noticed blood pooling on the table from these cuts, which is highly unusual. A cadaver at most would leak embalming fluid since the blood is extracted during the embalming process.

"I ran my finger on the skin and noticed grey powder coming off on my glove. It seemed someone had made the effort to mask the victim as a cadaver, but the exposed skin said otherwise. I checked her pulse to determine if she was alive, and then called nine-one-one."

Morris now turned to Zora. "Was this your first cadaver?"

Zora wrung her hands together but hid them

under the desk. "Yes, I got in here around seven-thirty to get a head start on the dissection."

"Aren't you supposed to be working in teams for this sort of thing?"

"Yes, we are. But my lab partners and I agreed yesterday I would go ahead and make the first cuts, since they're more squeamish than I am. They were going to join me at eight a.m."

"So what happened?"

"When I arrived, all the bodies were on the tables and covered with sheets. My team and I had been assigned our table, so I just headed there. I began the cuts not long after, since the body was already in the proper position."

"Did you notice anything unusual?" Morris asked.

"Not at first. There were no notable scars or marks. The body appeared a little bloated, and the victim's hair looked shiny, both which seemed unusual. But I haven't been around cadavers a lot, so I just assumed it was peculiar to this body."

"So what happened next?"

"I made the cuts, but then noticed blood was seeping from the incision edges. It was so unexpected that I ran up to the professor's office. I'd seen his car in the parking lot when I came in, so I assumed he'd be in his office. I told him something was wrong with the body. You already know what happened after that."

"Do you have cameras in the lab?" Morris asked Professor Braun.

"No, we don't, but we have one in the hallway," he responded.

Morris gave a quick nod to Shepherd, who left the room. Then he turned back to the professor. "Who normally has access to this section of the building?"

"The professors and staff, and medical students," Professor Braun replied. "We also have janitors—one per shift—who make sure that everything is locked up at the end of the day. Most folks are out of the building by nine p.m, but anyone can still enter the lab as long as their ID card has the permission neces- sary to do so."

"Do all medical students have access?"

"No. They all can enter the building, but only the first years can get into the lab. Staff who have permission to work in the lab can enter as well."

"Can we get a list of all those who can do so?"

"Sure. I can ask my secretary to give you a list."

The professor stood up and walked a few steps away. He pulled his phone from his lab coat pocket, dialed a number, and spoke to someone on the other end of the line.

Detective Shepherd poked his head through the open doorway. "Morris, I have the janitor here with me."

Morris waved them both in, and a man who seemed to be in his early sixties walked in behind Shepherd. He was dressed in green scrubs and had a scruffy, unkempt look about him with his unshaven beard and hair that looked like it hadn't seen a comb in a while.

"And you are ..." Detective Morris asked the newcomer.

"Pickles. Alfred Pickles," the man responded in an old tired voice.

Zora stifled a chuckle which turned into a snort at a stern look from Morris. She ducked her head and stared at her hands instead.

"So, Mr. Pickles, when did you arrive in the building today?" Detective Morris asked.

"I work night shifts from eight p.m. until eight a.m., so I've been here since last night. My replacement came in late, which is why I'm still around."

"Did you notice anything strange last night or this morning?"

"It was generally quiet." The man rubbed his

fingers along his jaw. "Although I saw someone in a hooded jacket coming out from the lab last night as I conducted my rounds."

Zora felt eyes on her and looked up to see the janitor staring at her with an expression that was unnerving. She shivered and glanced away.

"What time was this?" Morris asked.

The janitor turned back to Morris. "It was around nine p.m. I typically do my rounds at that time to make sure people have left the building." The man paused and cleared his throat. "That was when I saw the person in the hooded jacket coming out of the lab. Looked like a student. A female if you ask me, from her stature. I called out to her, but she took off running down the emergency stairs like she'd done something wrong.

"By the time I got to the door leading to the stairs, the person was long gone. I walked back and checked the lab but didn't notice anything amiss. I checked the other rooms on the floor, and nothing was unusual. I then made a note of it in my report, which I handed over to my colleague this morning."

"Anything else?" Morris asked Pickles.

The old man shook his head. "Nothing I can remember."

"Thanks for your help. Why don't you give your

contact details to Detective Shepherd? We'll get back to you if we have any additional questions. Here's my card in case you remember anything else."

The man nodded and took the proffered card, then walked with Shepherd to the door.

Zora noticed the man give her a final backward glance before exiting the room, a look Morris caught as well. Why did the old man stare at her like she'd done something wrong? She had a bad feeling about it, and suddenly felt the urge to leave and get as far away from the building as possible.

She rose to her feet. Zora's right leg had fallen asleep, and she tried to massage the feeling back into it. Her professor was still occupied on the phone, but she couldn't wait until he was done. "If there's nothing else, I'd like to leave," she said to Morris.

Morris regarded her with a cool gaze. It seemed to Zora like he'd made a quick judgment of her and found her lacking. "Okay," he said finally. "Make sure you leave your details as well with Detective Shepherd on your way out." He was about to say something else but seemed to hold himself back.

She gave him a quick nod and limped ungracefully toward the exit.

The door opened as she got closer. Detective Shepherd stepped in, walked past Zora, and whispered to Morris. Then the murmurs stopped, and she felt their eyes on her back, like they knew something she didn't.

Zora forced herself to remain calm and lifted her chin. Appearances were everything with the police, and she'd done nothing wrong.

So she squared her shoulders and held her head high as she left the room.

Zora leaned back on the couch in her apartment and closed her eyes. She was glad to be back home. This was her place of refuge. A haven for both her and Christina.

Christina was her best friend from childhood, and an ER nurse at the local hospital. Christina had moved in with her when Zora's mother expressed her displeasure at Zora living alone in town.

Painted in muted pink, adorned with pink and gold polka dot curtains, and furnished with a color-splattered couch and green plants, Zora's living room reflected how she'd always wanted her life to be—serene but full of color.

But right now, her life was a far cry from that.

4

Zora leaned back on the couch in her apartment and closed her eyes. She was glad to be back home. This was her place of refuge. A haven for both her and Christina.

Christina was her best friend from childhood, and an ER nurse at the local hospital. Christina had moved in with her when Zora's mother expressed her displeasure at Zora living alone in town.

Painted in muted pink, adorned with pink and gold polka dot curtains, and furnished with a color-splattered couch and green plants, Zora's living room reflected how she'd always wanted her life to be—serene but full of color.

But right now, her life was a far cry from that.

What had happened this morning had been scary. Her heart raced just thinking about it. A dead woman on her table. And she wasn't even a surgeon in the operating room yet.

The more she thought about it, the more Zora's hands shook, and she wrapped her arms around her body. She had flayed the victim's back and might have become a murderer if not that she'd arrived later than planned from making a stop at her favorite specialty coffee shop. She'd overheard the rumors from the other students that the medical examiner believed the victim died recently.

What if the woman had been alive when she'd started dissecting? Just the thought of it sent Zora's heart racing, and her breath came in sharp inhales. She could feel her mind beginning to spiral.

No! She couldn't afford a panic attack right now. Zora forced herself to take a series of deep breaths to fend it off, and after a few moments, her body responded.

She let out a sigh of relief. Crisis averted.

But Zora couldn't help thinking about the dead woman. Who was she? And who had placed her on Zora's table? Was it really a coincidence?

How had the killer gained access to the lab?

Everyone who entered the building had to use an approved key pass. What if it was a fellow medical student?

Zora shook her head. It was wrong of her to think of her colleagues as killers. They were in the business of learning how to save lives not take them.

Or was it an employee? So many what ifs and no answers.

Zora's head spun with all the questions, and she felt a headache coming on. She rubbed her temples as if to drive the pain away. Maybe she needed to forget about everything for now.

The shrill tone of her phone cut through the air. Zora tried to ignore it, but the phone kept ringing. She forced herself to sit up and reached for her bag on the coffee table before digging through it and finding her phone. A look at the caller ID showed it was her mother calling.

Zora rubbed her forehead. Her mother was the last person she wanted to talk to right now. But Zora knew her mother wouldn't stop calling until she answered, so she pressed the green button.

"Zora," her mother said from the other end of the line.

"Hello, Mother," Zora replied, her voice caustic. Her mother tended to bring out the worst in her.

"I heard there was a problem at school."

"Are you spying on me now?" she snapped. Zora couldn't help herself. Things had not been the same between her and her mother ever since her sister had been kidnapped. Zora blamed her for everything that had happened.

Her mother sighed. "It's all over the news, though they didn't say who found the body."

Zora grabbed the remote from the coffee table and switched on the TV. A reporter stood on the grass in front of a familiar red brick colonial building and talked about the body that had been discovered.

She let out an exhale. Zora's name hadn't been mentioned, but it was only a matter of time before the news hounds uncovered her role in it. This was the first time she could recall seeing her school on the news, and she knew the networks would milk it for all it was worth, which meant they would try and find out everything about the case. Including her.

"Are you okay?" her mother asked.

Zora had forgotten her mother was still on the line. She knew she needed to tell her about her involvement in the case, but she couldn't bring herself to do it. "Why wouldn't I be?" she retorted instead.

Her mother sighed on the other end of the line. "A

simple yes or no would have sufficed. I'm just checking to make sure you're okay."

Zora knew that was true, but the right words somehow fled her mind whenever her mother was concerned. Then she heard another voice in the background, and she sensed instinctively what her mother was about to say next.

"I have to go. I have a meeting now," her mother said. "I'll talk to you later, okay?" She didn't wait for Zora's response, and the line went dead.

Zora wanted to throw her phone across the room. Her mother elicited this response from her any time she mentioned going to a meeting. Not that there was anything wrong with meetings. Zora attended some herself. But that had always been her mother's excuse every time Zora had a competition in middle and high school, every time she'd needed her, and even when her sister had been kidnapped. Those words always cut her to the marrow. And her mother never stopped using them. As a result, their relationship remained on the rocks, and Zora didn't know how to change it.

She ran a hand through her hair. She didn't need this today, not with what had happened.

Zora flopped back on the couch and dropped her cellphone on the coffee table. Switching on the TV had been a bad idea—watching it had reminded her of what she'd been trying to forget.

And somehow she couldn't shake off the feeling that things were only going to get worse.

5

C alvin Faulkner removed his glasses, placed them on the desk, and rubbed his eyes. He was bone tired after working long hours for the past few days and needed a little rest. But that seemed like a luxury he couldn't afford right now.

He looked out through his slightly ajar office door and realized his secretary wasn't at her desk. She must have gone out for lunch—the only time Sarah Murray ever left her spot. How she got all the work done without stepping a foot away from her area was still a mystery. He checked the time on his Grand Seiko wristwatch. It was one p.m. His assumption was correct.

Sarah Murray never missed lunch. It was prime time to pump the other secretaries and assistants in the company for morsels of gossip. Calvin had found out about this favorite pastime of hers after she'd transferred to his office. Of course, he'd benefited from her hobby a time or two, but that didn't mean he approved of it. After all, she must have shared gossip about him in return.

Calvin grimaced as his stomach growled. He hadn't eaten anything all day, and it was too late to head to the cafeteria. Maybe Sarah would grab something for him to eat. She sometimes did, but it was totally on her whim. Anyway, food had to wait for now, considering all that he had on his *plate*.

He looked down on the piles of paper strewn everywhere on his desk and sighed. Calvin still had a long way to go with the deal he was working on, and he had a meeting with the other party in three days. Most of the deal terms had been locked in, but there were two critical areas that needed to be hashed out for the deal to be worthwhile. And Calvin was shooting for it to be highly profitable. That meant he had to be prepared for every eventuality. This deal could net him a generous bonus and a chance to move from this generic office—only big enough to fit his brown oak desk and two black swivel chairs—to a much larger office on the twelfth floor with huge windows and spacious dimensions.

It would be a glorious day indeed when that happened.

Calvin ran a hand through his dark wavy hair. His colleagues would say he wasn't particularly handsome with his beak-like nose and thin set lips that curled easily into a frown, but his physique more than made up for what he lacked in beauty and charisma. Calvin worked out religiously, kept his body in top form, and made sure he wore the right clothes to complement it. Today he was wearing a grey custom Italian suit with a white crisp cotton shirt and a pair of black Stefano Bemer shoes. He'd received multiple compliments from the ladies in the office on his way in, but he wasn't interested in any of them—they had neither money nor connections. And he needed both.

He heard a knock on his door and looked up to see Tom Cavanaugh poking his head into the office. Calvin had first met Tom on a previous deal where Calvin had been the external counsel and hadn't yet been employed by the company. Tom was also his first friend after he'd joined.

Tom pushed the door open and strode in without waiting for a response, shutting the door behind him. The smell of bacon followed him in as he squeezed his bulky frame into the black swivel chair opposite Calvin. Tom was unassuming, with curly brown hair, a double-chinned face, and a pendulous belly that was a testament to how much he loved eating fried chicken. He'd never missed a day at the cafeteria for as long as Calvin had known him.

Calvin tried to mask his annoyance. He wasn't really up for a visit, but there was no point in telling Tom he was busy. He wouldn't leave until he'd said his piece.

"Have you heard?" Tom said.

"Heard what?"

"Martha Adams in HR is dead. She was murdered."

Calvin arched one eyebrow. "Murdered?"

"Yes, she was found at the Lexinbridge Medical School lab. It was all over the news in the cafeteria."

Calvin leaned back. He remembered her. Skinny, with a forgettable face and a voice that tended to grate on the nerves. She was constantly going on and on about one diet or the other. Not that any of it would have enhanced her chances of scoring with the opposite sex—her attitude made sure of that. She was a notorious complainer, and after working with her for a week, he'd been about ready to pull out his hair. He got the sense she wasn't really liked in the office, but he doubted it was to the point where she would have been murdered for it.

"Too bad for her," he muttered. He looked at his friend suspiciously. "Why are you telling me this?"

"You guys seemed to have been joined at the hip last year."

Calvin gave a sardonic laugh. "Me? And Martha Adams?"

"Seriously. I thought you guys were dating. When I stopped seeing you together, I figured the flame had fizzled out, so I didn't bother asking about it."

Calvin gave Tom a stern look. "Are you trying to insult me by any chance?"

Tom held up his hands in mock surrender. "Hey, no need to get pissy at me." He fiddled with his tie. How he managed to get it around his fat neck was anyone's guess. "It's a pity she's dead."

"A pity indeed," Calvin agreed.

"Anyway, I just came to tell you about it." Tom dragged himself upright. The chair groaned as if ready to fall apart. "I gotta go. I'm off for a meeting. Later."

Calvin didn't hear Tom leave. His thoughts were already on that fateful day with Martha.

It had been a terrible affair, and he regretted his involvement in it. Just remembering it still made him grit his teeth. But it had turned into a great opportunity, one he hadn't hesitated to take advantage of. Anyone else would have done the same.

He sighed. All of that didn't concern him anymore. It was in the past, and there was no reason for it to be related to Martha's death.

Calvin chucked it out of his mind and turned his attention back on the papers on his desk.

It was time to wrap up this deal.

6

Zora was lost in her thoughts until she heard the key turn in the lock. The front door opened, and Christina walked in. Petite with the most gorgeous red hair, Christina was a sight for sore eyes. People always wondered how they could be friends since they were polar opposites— Zora was tall and curvy with wavy dark hair and was more reserved, while Christina was a born extrovert.

Christina set down her keys and bag on the black granite kitchen countertop and walked over to the couch where she dropped herself next to Zora. Her soft lilac scent filled the air and Zora's nostrils.

"You're back," Zora said. She'd remained on the couch after the call with her mother and had somehow lost track of time. She could see the dying rays of the sun peek through the curtains.

"I'm so exhausted," Christina responded, letting out a big yawn as she kicked off her shoes. "How was your day?"

Zora sighed. "A nightmare."

Christina gave Zora a sharp look. "What do you mean? I thought you were starting Gross Anatomy lab today. And I know you've been looking forward to it."

"Didn't you see the news?"

"What news? My shift was so busy I didn't even have time to catch my breath. What did I miss?"

"A murder."

Christina sat up abruptly. "A murder? How did that happen? Are you okay?" Her stunning green eyes searched Zora's face.

"I'm okay, or I think I am." Zora then told Christina everything that had happened at the lab.

Christina's mouth hung open. "Unbelievable! Seriously though, are you okay?"

"I really don't know how I feel." Zora rubbed her eyes. "But I can't seem to get it out of my mind." She fingered the pendant on the gold necklace around her neck.

Christina placed a hand on Zora's arm. "This was

a pretty traumatic experience for you, you know," she said softly. "Have you thought about seeing your therapist?"

Zora gave her a harsh look. "That's not going to happen."

"But Zora, I'm just afraid—"

"I mean it. I'm not going back there. You know how it was when my sister disappeared. And I've sworn off all therapists since then. I'm not going through that again." Zora got up. "You know what? I'm going to take a shower and head to bed. I'll probably feel better when I wake up in the morning."

"Won't you eat dinner?"

"I'm not hungry." She picked up her phone from the coffee table and made for her room, feeling Christina's eyes on her the whole way.

Christina was right to be worried, but Zora was going to handle it just fine on her own.

And better than last time.

The cadaver on the table had no scars on its body. Zora ran her hand down its back—it was smooth to the touch. Perfect. She picked up her scalpel from the stainless-steel surgical bowl and made a horizontal shoulder-to-shoulder cut on the body. As she was about to make a vertical cut down its spine, the cadaver snapped its head to the left and stared straight at Zora.

Zora shrieked, and the scalpel clattered from her hand and fell on the dissecting table. Her heart pounded against her chest as she stumbled backward and almost fell on her backside.

A face that looked like her sister's stared back at her from the cadaver. It opened its mouth and let out a keening wail.

Zora grabbed her chest as the sound pierced her like a hot knife and scorched her insides. Her skittish heart threatened to burst from her ribcage as if fleeing from the intensity of the heat. She scrambled backward and didn't feel any pain when her back hit the leg of another dissecting table behind her. Zora's chest rose and fell rapidly, desperate for fresh oxygen like a drowning man, and she pressed her hands hard against her ears to block out the sound.

The cadaver sat up with its legs dangling from the side of the table and continued to stare at Zora with soulless blue eyes. Blood dripped from its back onto the table in rivulets. As she huddled under the table, Zora watched the blood spread and cover the cadaver's hands that rested on the table's surface.

She screamed again.

Her eyes jerked open. Zora's pulse raced, and her heart beat furiously in her rib cage. She was back on her bed, her hair limp with sweat, and her sheets wrapped around her in disarray. The air felt oppressive, and darkness choked the room.

Zora stumbled out of bed and rushed into the shower. She crouched in the corner of the stall as water from the rain shower head streamed around her.

She lost track of how long she stayed there, mumbling Psalm Twenty-Three over and over again until she felt her heart slow down to a more regular pace and the knot in her stomach relax. Zora's grandmother had taught her the psalm when she was just a little girl, and it had always been a solace to her whenever she had nightmares. It didn't fail her this time either.

Zora dragged herself out of the shower and stripped off her wet clothes. She toweled herself dry, ran the hair dryer through her hair, and changed into fresh sleepwear. Zora straightened her sheets, and then crawled back under the covers.

She checked the time. It was just eleven p.m. She still had a long way to go before morning, and there was no guarantee she would fall back asleep.

Zora cringed at the thought of what was to come. The nightmares would never let up and would run her ragged until the cause of the distress was resolved. It was like a warning sign—it had been that way ever since her sister was kidnapped. In this case, it was because of the dead victim she'd discovered on her table in the lab.

The murderer needed to be found quickly if she was to maintain her sanity and find peace again. Things had gone worse for her in the past whenever she'd ignored the nightmare and didn't do anything about what had triggered it. Zora wasn't ready to make the same mistake again—the outcome would be far worse this time around.

There was one person who could help her, and Zora resolved to reach out to him the next day.

With the decision made, sleep came quickly.

7

Drake Pierce leaned back on his plush black leather swivel chair and folded his arms across his chest. It had been a long week so far attending useless departmental meetings, and he was ready to call it a day. He didn't understand why his old man insisted he attend all of them. After all, those employees were paid to make money for him and his family, and he didn't see any sense in handholding them. If they couldn't live up to their responsibilities, then they needed to go—there were many more willing to take their spots.

He got up and walked over to the floor-to-ceiling windows that displayed the beautiful skyline of Lexinbridge. The sun receded in the horizon, casting its red-orange glow on rows of towering glittering skyscrapers interspersed by city-planted blooms. This was his city, and he planned to own every corner of it. Money ruled here, and Drake's bank accounts were bursting at the seams.

The years spent investing in risky deals had paid off. Drake had spent the money expanding his influence in the city. Everyone had a price and could be bought. No one was immune to it. Even the politicians—who were incentivized to keep their hands clean or else face jail time—were susceptible. They all had weaknesses, and Drake had learned to exploit them. Now all he had to do was bid his time until his old man croaked and he inherited the company.

He had to admit his father was smart. It was no surprise since Drake had gotten his money-making qualities from him. But his father was limited by his archaic views. Drake didn't see anything wrong with skirting around the edges of the law. He would never be caught—he was that careful. And even if he was exposed, he could afford the best lawyers money could buy, and the judges were already in his pocket.

Drake could see, reflected in the window, his Adonis looks that the ladies adored—sun-kissed wavy hair that curled up at the base of his neck, a chiseled symmetrical jaw line, piercing blue eyes, a smile that made the girls swoon, and a lean build accentuated by a light blue dress shirt and grey three-piece suit with matching burgundy silk tie and pocket square, topped off with diamond-encrusted gold cuff links. It didn't help he'd graduated with a major in Finance from NYU, followed by an MBA at Harvard. The ladies clamored and sold themselves for a chance to be with him. All he had to do was flick a finger, and they would come running. He was, of course, happy to oblige their wishes, and even then, he always remained in control.

Except for that one time when he hadn't been able to help himself. Her pale blue innocent eyes had drawn him in and awakened the animal in him.

Drake shook his head to drive the thought away. It was a time he didn't want to remember, but only because cleaning up the ensuing mess had made him vulnerable to those who helped him. And that was a position in which he didn't plan to put himself ever again.

He was lucky his father hadn't figured it out. Of course the old man had his suspicions, but there was no evidence. It would have been the perfect excuse to cut Drake off from the company, which his father would have done. The old man was brutal that way. He made no allowances for anyone, not even his son.

If Drake didn't know better, he would have thought he was adopted.

Drake couldn't allow his hard work to be in vain —not now and not in the future. He had to be more careful. His old man had eyes and ears everywhere, and Drake needed to stay under the radar until the firm became his.

He ran his hands through his blond hair. It was time to let loose. A trip to the H Club was in order. Drake had heard about the new girl, Susie, and he needed to see for himself if she lived up to expectations. If she did, then she would be perfect for tonight's exercise. Just thinking about it got his blood flowing.

Drake walked back to his desk and pressed a hidden button beneath its surface. His bodyguard, Tiny, knocked on his frosted glass door and stepped in. Tiny filled the entrance of his office with his wide muscled build and tree-trunk legs. Drake had saved Tiny five years ago from life imprisonment, and Tiny had sworn allegiance to him at the time. They'd been together ever since.

"Let's go to the H Club," Drake said.

The night was about to get interesting.

8

P rofessor James Oakley exited the elevator at the basement floor of the Genetics building and walked into the darkened parking lot. It'd been a long day, and he was exhausted. The parking garage's hidden motion detectors triggered the lights as his long legs ate up the distance to his car. The vehicle, a BMW E30 M3 Coupe, winked at him from the far right corner of the garage.

Seeing his car always made his heart race. It had been an impulse buy many years ago right before his career started its meteoric rise. He loved everything about it from its salmon-silver metallic color and supple all-black leather interior, to its boxy body form which hid a powerful straight-four engine under the hood. He had maintained it religiously over the years, and the car shone in response. It was still as gorgeous today as it had been the day he'd bought it. He considered the car his good luck charm—his career had accelerated beyond his wildest dreams since its purchase, making him the envy of all his colleagues.

Professor Oakley glanced at his watch and frowned. He was already very late. He'd promised his wife he would be home in time for dinner. She'd told him this morning that she would be making her special chicken-beef lasagna—his favorite dish, one that he never missed. The mere thought had made him postpone any meetings today that could have derailed his dinner plans. But the unexpected had happened.

His secretary had received an unmarked envelope delivered for him this afternoon. Professor Oakley had tried to track down the courier service that had delivered the envelope, but the courier company had confirmed they hadn't sent a package to him today.

He'd torn open the envelope in haste, and a single photo had dropped out. A picture he'd hidden in the safe behind the wood panel in his office.

Professor Oakley could never forget the day the picture was taken. After a particularly tiresome day, he'd headed to the local hotel for drinks at the bar. It was a ritual he'd started while in grad school and which he'd maintained over the years. After a few drinks, he'd been ready to head home when he'd met a young lady in her twenties. She was called Laura and had said she was a graduate student at the university with a strong interest in genetics. It wasn't everyday he saw a lady with both beauty and knowledge of a topic he loved.

They'd chatted over more drinks, and the next thing he knew, he'd opened his eyes to see himself lying naked on a bed next to a different girl—nude and clearly underaged. A rotund man with tattoos peeking out of his collar had been taking pictures of him. That was when it dawned on him that his drinks had been spiked. But it had been too late to do anything about it. The pictures would ruin his career and marriage, and the police would never believe he hadn't slept with the minor.

The blackmails had started that day, and he'd been paying them off ever since. But there had been no issues, as he always made his payments on time. So he hadn't expected one of the pictures to surface again today.

He'd been so frazzled by the photo that he'd forgotten the presentation paper he'd been putting together for a conference in a few weeks. By the time he'd remembered the paper he was going to present at the Annual Meeting of the American Society of Human Genetics, the day was far spent. Since he needed to send off the paper soon, Professor Oakley had doubled down in the last three hours to finish it. And now he was late for dinner.

He looked around the garage and realized it was almost empty. The section of the parking lot he was now in had poor lighting. The air was still, and shadows danced around the bare cement pillars and dark corners. The ongoing major renovations in this area made it look like a mini war zone.

Professor Oakley shivered, a sense of apprehension enveloping him. Even though the air felt nippy, he wondered if he was cold for another reason.

He'd heard the news about the murder case in the Gross Anatomy lab in a different section of the campus. Fortunately, Professor Oakley hadn't known the victim. But now, most folks in the campus were scared. It was all they'd talked about today at the end of meetings and in the cafeteria. Everyone was wondering if they would be the next victim. So the campus had emptied out earlier than normal. No one wanted to be around if a killer was on the prowl, including him. It was best he hurried home.

Professor Oakley hastened his steps until he

reached the driver's side of his car. He pulled his keys from his pocket and fumbled with them a bit before he finally managed to unlocked the door. Professor Oakley slid into the car, dropped his leather satchel on the passenger seat, and shut the door.

He let out a sigh of relief. He was safe now.

As he turned the key in the ignition to start the car, a shadow rose from the back seat behind him and plunged a needle into his neck.

Professor Oakley's eyes widened in fear, and he reached up to pull out the needle. The needle clattered to the floor of the back seat.

The assailant spread his gloved hands around Professor Oakley's neck and squeezed.

Professor Oakley clawed at the hands to get them off his throat, his knees hitting the steering wheel as he fought for his chance to breathe.

But the assailant didn't let up, and eventually, Professor Oakley weakened—much faster than he would have expected for a man like him who jogged every day. His eyes widened as he realized his brain was losing control over his limbs. He'd been injected with a muscle relaxant!

His heart rate spiked, and Professor Oakley became more frantic in a last ditch effort to free himself. But it was to no avail. His limbs dropped like heavy weights to his sides.

The assailant whispered something into his ear, his breath heavy and foul. Professor Oakley's eyes widened in shock. He tried to form words but couldn't.

The last thing he saw was his life slipping away before the darkness claimed him.

Leonard Frisk, fondly known as Leo, had been a security guard at Lexinbridge Medical School for thirty-five years. It was a good job, and the only troubles were the occasional car lockout or lost parking ticket.

But Leo was looking forward to his retirement at the end of the week. He'd promised his wife, Betty, that they would take a cruise for their thirtieth wedding anniversary in two weeks. Betty was especially looking forward to it—it had always been a dream of theirs. She deserved it for sticking with him all these years. It would be their first out-of-state trip since they got married, and Leo was excited about the adventure.

Leo shivered and rubbed his short arms as he

walked through the parking lot of the Genetics building. The air was a bit chilly, and the short sleeves of his security uniform did nothing to help. He hated the cold. His bald head hated it too. So he was eager to head to warmer weather for the cruise. Fortunately, his morning round through the parking lot was usually quick. He would be done in a jiffy and back to the security room in no time to drink the flask of black coffee Betty kindly made for him every morning. Leo quickened his steps at the thought of the hot liquid.

As he circled back to finish the loop around the garage, he noticed a head resting on the steering wheel of Professor Oakley's car. Professor Oakley had parked in the same spot for over ten years, so Leo recognized his car at first glance.

That's strange, he thought. He'd never seen Professor Oakley this way, and he wondered what was wrong.

Leo moved closer to the driver's side and knocked on the window. "Professor Oakley?"

There was no response. The head remain motionless on the steering wheel.

Leo rapped his knuckles on the window again. "Professor?"

There was still no reaction.

Leo felt a strong sense of foreboding come over him. The Martha Adams case had put everyone on high alert, and the higher-ups had mentioned in the meeting yesterday that the campus couldn't afford another dead body. Leo hoped the professor was alright and had only slept off.

He walked around to the passenger side to see if he could get the professor's attention. That was when he saw the eyes staring blankly at him through the window, arms hanging awkwardly to the sides. He didn't need a doctor to tell him Professor Oakley was dead.

Knowing that the chance of a cruise in the near future was gone until the case was solved, and swallowing the bile that rose to his throat, Leo lifted his radio to his mouth and called the campus police.

9

Zora woke up to the sunlight filtering in through the curtains into her room. She was bone tired, and her head ached. The nightmare had not repeated itself again in the night, and for that she was grateful. She turned her head to check the time on the alarm clock on her bedside table and saw she was already late for class.

"Oh, shoot!" Zora sprang up from her bed and rushed into the bathroom. She took a quick shower and dressed hurriedly in a white blouse and grey slacks. She was late for her Immunology class at eight a.m., and the professor frowned sternly on latecomers.

Zora ran a brush through her hair and tied it up in a ponytail, then grabbed her book bag from her desk, tossed her phone from the bedside table into it, and rushed out of the room.

The smell of freshly toasted bread greeted her as she stepped into the living area. Christina was already awake and was lounging in a white graphic T-shirt and pink shorts at the kitchen countertop, munching on some toast and scrambled eggs. The curtains had been pulled to the sides, and the living room was awash with light.

"Morning," Christina said. "You look terrible. Where are you off to?"

"Good morning to you too," Zora responded. "Thanks for the compliment, but I gotta go. I'm late for Immunology class. Ouch!" She'd stumped her big toe at the edge of the couch and now rubbed her toe to make the ache go away. Then she limped to the door to grab her shoes. "I'll see you later."

"You do know it's Saturday, right?" Christina said, her eyes twinkling with mirth, as Zora opened the door to step out.

Zora turned and closed the door. "Why didn't you tell me earlier?"

Christina grinned and took another bite of her toast.

Zora dropped her book bag in front of the door,

rushed to where Christina was sitting, grabbed her from behind, and began to tickle her.

"I'm sorry! I'm sorry!" Christina said over and over again as she tried to twist away from Zora and escape her hands. Zora eventually let her go and grabbed her remaining toast.

Christina moaned. "Hey! That was the last one."

"Make yourself another," Zora said as she scarfed down the toast.

Christina sat back on the stool and took a sip of her coffee. Her eyes searched Zora's face. "How are we doing today? Did you sleep well last night?"

Zora said nothing and continued chewing. Christina knew about her nightmares but never asked about them unless Zora brought one up. Zora decided she wouldn't mention it today.

Christina waited and continued sipping her coffee.

"I'm okay," Zora finally responded. Though Christina said nothing, Zora could see from her gaze she didn't believe her.

Her phone rang at that moment and cut through the awkwardness in the air. Zora left the kitchen and strode to the door to pick up her book bag. She rummaged through it until she found her phone and glanced at the screen. She didn't recognize the number, but she hit the answer button anyway.

"This is Zora Smyth."

"Miss Smyth, this is Detective Morris from the Lexinbridge Police Station. We have some additional questions for you. Would it be possible for you to come down to the station today?"

Zora's day was mostly free. "Sure, I can come down this afternoon," she answered as she walked back to the kitchen. Christina gave Zora a curious glance.

"Okay. Let me know when you get here," Morris said before disconnecting the call.

Zora tossed her phone down on the kitchen countertop.

"What was that all about?" Christina asked.

"It's the detective from yesterday. He wants me to come down to the station to answer some questions."

10

Thomas Strickland had always been Zora's classmate. They'd attended the same middle school, high school, and college, and had ended up in the same medical school.

Talk about bad luck. Zora always ended up first in class, while Thomas seemed to have an eternal claim to second place, which meant Zora always got the merit scholarships that Thomas craved. It wouldn't have hurt so bad if Zora hadn't come from a wealthy home.

Everyone in school had known she was privileged —her mother was a notable figure in Lexinbridge. So Zora didn't need the scholarships. On the other hand, Thomas had had no parents to rely on—his father was a mechanic by day and a drunkard by night. His mother had long abandoned their home. He'd never had enough growing up and had worked three jobs to put himself through college. Now it seemed the nightmare was about to repeat itself.

Thomas desperately needed funds to stay in medical school. The external funds he'd been able to garner were not enough to cover his expenses. A friend of his had convinced him to try to double what little money he had at the blackjack table, and Thomas had lost that too. Now he was really in a bind. If he didn't make tuition payments soon, he would have to take the year off. All his previous hard work would be in vain, and the time off would be a negative strike on his profile, hindering his chance for a good placement for residency and fellowship. So Thomas needed a solution immediately.

Zora and Thomas had both applied for a highly sought-after scholarship recently. Not only would the winner get thirty thousand dollars, but their books and housing costs would be covered as well. It didn't hurt that it would also look good on the resumé, which would be advantageous for future scholarships and residency placements. Winning it would ease Thomas' financial woes and place him in a good spot. But Thomas had heard from one of the financial office assistants, who had a crush on him, that he was placed second after Zora.

He could see his dream slipping away if he didn't do something about it. By chance, Thomas had been in the Gross Anatomy building the night before, and had seen Zora coming out of the lab. He'd seen someone else too, but hadn't recognized the person even though he could tell it was a man—a hood had hidden his face. Thomas had noticed that both Zora and the man were wearing hooded jackets and were about the same height.

Thomas was desperate and felt he had no choice. He knew if he pointed the finger at Zora, she would become a suspect. All he had to do was whisper it into the right ears, and the news would spread like wildfire. Mrs. Mutton at the library was an example of the perfect candidate. Maybe he could even drop an anonymous note at the financial office to nudge the rumor in the right direction. Zora would then become ineligible for the scholarship, opening up the opportunity for him to take her place.

He felt a prick to his conscience for what he planned to do, but he reasoned that Zora could afford those high-profile lawyers that could get anyone out of a bind—she would come out of the situation as clean as a whistle. And she wouldn't miss the scholarship. He, on the other hand, deserved it after all these years. Yes, he did.

But first he needed the rumors to spring from the one place that would legitimize them.

So he called the police station and asked for the detective on the case. When he came on the line, Thomas told him he had something "interesting" to tell him.

11

Z ora entered the police station and made her way to the reception area. The strong scents of cigarette smoke, unwashed bodies, and air freshener battled for dominance in the room. As her heels clicked on the polished concrete tiles and stopped in front of a glass partition, a burly male officer with a blank face looked up at her through the glass.

"How may I help you?" he asked.

"I'm here to see Detective Morris. He's expecting me."

"Hold on," he said. He picked up the telephone on the desk and dialed an extension.

Zora looked around the room while she waited. There were only two other visitors in the waiting area, and one had her eyes peeled on the secure door on the right as if waiting for someone to come through. There was an enlarged map of the city of Lexinbridge that dominated the wall on the left, right above a water fountain.

"He'll be with you shortly," the officer said as he replaced the receiver.

Zora nodded and walked back to sit in one of the chairs in the waiting area. She tried to adjust the position of the chair, but noticed it was bolted to the floor. Looking around, she realized they all were. She made herself as comfortable as she could, but the smell of cigarettes from the clothing of the only person seated in the waiting room assaulted her nose, and she couldn't hold back a cough.

"Miss Smyth?"

Zora looked up to see Detective Morris standing before her in a grey shirt with the sleeves rolled up and his tie askew. She'd missed the sound of the electronic door clicking open into the waiting room. She stood up and noticed she still had to look up to him at her height. His face revealed nothing.

"Thanks for coming," he continued. "This way please."

Zora followed him through the secure electronic door into the station. As the door closed behind her, she felt a claustrophobic sensation wash over her. Sweat trickled down her back with every step she took down the hallway. She almost turned to flee the station, but she forced herself to move forward. If she ran now, she would look suspicious. *Heaven knows how the detectives would interpret that*, she thought.

The air buzzed with the sound of keyboards clicking, phones ringing, dispatchers speaking into headsets, and printers spewing out rap sheets. The smell of aged coffee and stale pizza filled Zora's nostrils as they passed the break room.

Morris stopped in front of one of the rooms on the left and led the way in. The medium-sized cream-colored room was windowless, but there was a large mirror positioned about five feet high on one side of the wall. Zora guessed the mirror was two-way—it couldn't have been there for decorative purposes. She wondered if there was anyone on the other side.

Yellow light washed the room from the recessed bulb in the center of the ceiling, and Zora noticed two cameras discreetly hidden in the top corners of the room. There was a table bolted to the floor in the center of the room, and three chairs surrounded it. Detective Shepherd was already seated in one of the chairs with some papers arranged on the table in front of him. Morris folded himself into the empty chair next to Shepherd and motioned for Zora to sit in the remaining one.

As Zora sat down and crossed her legs, a slight chill ran through her. The whole scenario smacked of an interrogation. She'd thought she was just supposed to answer a few questions and now realized too late that if they only had simple questions for her, they could have asked her on the phone or stopped by her classes.

"Just to make sure we capture the information accurately, we're going to record this conversation. This is Detective Morris of the Lexinbridge Police Department speaking, with Detective Shepherd also present. Could you please state your name for us?"

This was bad sign number two. There was something the detectives were not telling her.

Zora uncrossed and crossed her legs. "Do I need my lawyer present?" she asked.

"Miss Smyth, this is just a friendly chat and won't take long. We only have some additional questions for you."

Against her better judgment, Zora decided to go along with it. She figured if she resisted now, it might work against her. She could stop the questioning at any time. "Okay, this is Zora Smyth."

"As in S-M-Y-T-H, correct?"

"Yes."

"Can I have your address, please?"

"111 Lakewood Drive, Lexinbridge."

"Okay. Do you need any water?"

"No, I'm good. Could we get to it already?"

"Sure." Morris pulled his little notebook from his pocket and consulted it. "We checked the CCTV from the day before, and we saw a young lady leaving the lab late in the evening. A witness confirmed it was you. Could you tell us why you were there?"

Zora stiffened. Someone had gone out of their way to point a finger at her. She wondered who. She'd indeed been at the lab the night before, but only to familiarize herself with the place.

"Miss Smyth?"

Zora came back to herself. "Yes?"

"Why were you at the lab that night?"

"I wanted to check out the place and make sure the body was in the right position for the next day's work."

Morris scribbled something in his notebook. "Couldn't you have done it in the morning?"

"If I needed to turn the body myself, some of the embalming fluid might get all over me, and I didn't want the smell to follow me to my other classes that day. I figured if I went at night, I could still take a shower, change my clothes, and have enough time for the smell to go away before the next day."

Morris nodded and made some further notes in his notebook. "We noticed you were wearing a hooded jacket. Why was that?"

"It was cold that night, and it was really just the first jacket I grabbed from my closet."

"So why did you run away?"

"I heard a noise that frightened me as I was coming out of the lab. I was scared. I didn't think it was a good idea to wait around and find out what the noise was. So I left."

"So why didn't you tell us you were at the lab the day before?"

"You didn't ask, and I didn't think it was relevant. After all, a lot of other students might have been there before and after I was at the lab."

"What was your relationship with Professor Oakley?"

"Professor who?"

"Professor Oakley, the genetics professor? We heard you had a clash with him recently."

Zora's heart picked up its pace. "What has that got to do with anything, or with this case?"

"Where were you last night?"

Zora looked at Shepherd and then at Morris. She swallowed. "Why do you ask?"

"Is there anyone that can vouch for your whereabouts last night?"

"Am I a suspect?" Zora asked. The detectives didn't answer. She folded her arms. "I want my lawyer."

As if on cue, the door flung open, and Silas Park strode in. Zora had never been so glad to see him.

Silas Park was her mother's number two guy. He was a well-known criminal lawyer who'd won some of the most notorious cases in town, despite being only about fifteen years older than Zora. He was clad as usual in an expensive grey three-piece suit, a white shirt, and a Harvard classic red twill tie—it made no difference whether it was a weekday or weekend. Zora was surprised to see him, but Silas just winked at her.

He headed to the table and placed his custom Italian leather briefcase on it, then turned to the detectives. "My client has nothing more to say. Are there any charges against her?"

"No," Morris responded.

"Then my client is free to leave at this time."

"Yes, she can go, but we'll probably call her again soon."

Silas ignored his response. He turned to Zora. "Come on, let's go."

Zora got up and followed Silas out of the interrogation room, and then the police station. As they stood on the steps leading into the station, Zora turned to Silas. "How did you know I was here?"

"You have to thank Christina for that. Christina thought something was wrong and called your mother, who then asked me to come." Silas cast a stern look at her. "But Zora, you should have known better than to come to the police station alone."

"I just thought—"

"Never ever do it again. Your mother taught you better."

Zora bristled at the mention of her mother. "And where is Mommy Dearest?"

"She had an important meeting and couldn't make it."

Zora was gutted and looked away. It was always the same with her mother. Her work was number one, and Zora was number two. Her sister's disappearance hadn't changed her, so how had Zora expected her to make an exception with her at the police station? Still, that didn't stop Zora from being disappointed with her.

Silas put a comforting hand on her shoulder. "You know she would be here if she could," he said softly.

Zora looked at him. "I know you're trying to make me feel better."

Silas gave her a sad smile, but Zora looked away. She didn't need any pity.

"I'm going to find out what's going on with this case and let you know," he said. "Let me take care of everything from here on. We won't let anything happen to you. In the meantime, don't talk to anyone about it. You know the drill."

Zora certainly remembered it. She'd gone through a similar experience when her sister disappeared. No discussion of the case with classmates, neighbors, police, or reporters. Not with anyone for that matter.

She was glad Silas would be on top of things, but that didn't stop her from worrying about being a possible suspect. This was clearly different from how things had been yesterday.

Why would they even think she was a potential murderer? Zora disliked death of any kind and even hated killing bugs. Why was this happening to her?

"So where do you want to go now?" Silas asked, drawing her out of her introspection.

There was only one place Zora wanted to be. "Home."

12

Zora stepped into her apartment and dropped her bag on the coffee table. For some reason, the bag felt heavier than when she'd carried it earlier today, and her body ached. It was good to be back home, and thankfully, she had the place to herself—Christina had left a message that she'd gone in for work.

Something about this place always called to Zora. Maybe because it was a place all her own and had its own personality, evidenced by the magenta-colored kitchen with its contrasting white cabinets and black granite countertop. The apartment had looked that way when Zora's eyes first fell on it, and she'd seen no need to change it.

Zora inhaled deeply, her sensitive nose twitching at the lingering fresh scent of exotic coffee and cinnamon, and she felt the heaviness in her chest dissipate. She'd been right to come straight home.

She padded into the kitchen and opened the refrigerator. The top and middle shelves were stacked with yoghurts and sealed containers of baked goods, cooked rice, beans, meat, vegetables, and soups. Zora could see Christina was at it again—she tended to cook up a storm whenever she was worried. Zora was worried about herself too. At least they wouldn't starve anytime soon.

Zora grabbed a bottle of water from the door of the refrigerator and closed it. Being in strange places made her thirsty, and the police station had definitely been one of those. She emptied the bottle, rinsed it in the sink, and refilled it from the tap. There was no point in buying a fresh bottle of water when she could recycle.

She placed the bottle back in the refrigerator and headed to the living room, where she sagged into the couch and closed her eyes for a brief respite.

But Zora couldn't stop thinking about what was happening to her. How had she gone from being the person who reported the incident to a potential suspect? What motive could she possibly have had to kill the woman? There was nothing connecting them except she'd been the first person to find her—she was an absolute stranger as far as Zora was concerned. Zora also valued life as one who hoped to become a surgeon, and the thought of harming anyone made her sick. She honestly didn't understand why the police were looking at her.

She fingered the pendant at her neck. Who was the witness, and why had he or she gone out of their way to point her out to the cops? Zora wasn't the friendliest person to be around, but she was almost sure she didn't have any enemies. She generally treated people well even if she didn't agree with them.

And what were those questions about Professor Oakley? Did he have anything to do with this? Disagreeing with a professor wasn't a new thing and was common enough on campus. In fact, the administration encouraged students to express themselves, and Zora had obliged.

Her phone rang. She sat up, rummaged through her bag for it, and looked at the screen. It was Silas.

"Hello, Silas," Zora said after she tapped the answer button.

"Hi, Zora. I just spoke with my contact at the police, and he confirmed you're being considered a potential suspect given your ties to both the victim and Professor Oakley."

Zora jumped up. "But I'm not connected to the victim. I only found her!"

"I know. But a witness came forward this morning and fingered you as having spent some time in the lab last night and hinted it was highly unusual and suspicious."

"That's hogwash!" Zora said as she strode back and forth across the living room.

"And the same witness mentioned you had an argument with Professor Oakley recently."

"What the ... This is nonsense! And who is this witness anyway?"

"I tried to find out the name of the witness, but Detective Morris had it pretty locked down," Silas said. "He's the only one aware of the witness' identity."

"So what's this about Professor Oakley?"

"Zora ... Professor Oakley was found murdered this morning. And the evidence seems to indicate it might be the same killer. Formalin and Rohypnol were found in the bloodstreams of both victims."

"Formalin? That's dangerous stuff!"

"I know. And it's easily obtainable."

"And why would the killer have used Rohypnol? Was there any evidence of sexual assault on the victims?"

"That's what's so strange. There was none."

Zora continued pacing. "This is ridiculous, you know. Why would I be the one to discover the body if I was the killer?"

"Zora, it's going to be alright," Silas tried to reassure her. "They don't have any direct evidence that ties you to both victims, so they can't charge you. And besides, you didn't do it."

Zora stopped pacing. "Thanks for the vote of confidence."

"You're welcome. Remember, we're on your side, and we won't let anything happen to you. It's going to be fine. I'll keep trying to see if I can find out the name of the witness. Let's stay in touch, okay?"

"Thanks for everything."

"Anytime. I'll talk to you later."

"Okay." Zora ended the call and dropped her phone on the coffee table.

This was getting worse. Now there were two

victims. She wondered if there was anything on the news about Professor Oakley, so she picked up the remote and switched the TV on.

Zora stared at the fifty-inch screen. The same baby-faced chubby reporter from the day before was standing in what looked like a parking garage and was reporting about a new murder case. Zora could see the familiar crime scene tape in the background cordoning off an area around a silver car.

"A certain professor of genetics, Professor James Oakley was found dead in his car this morning," the reporter said.

Seeing it on the news suddenly made it more real. Zora moved closer to hear more.

"The professor may have been murdered by the same killer who took Martha Adams' life a few days ago. We believe it's not a coincidence that the two victims died in the same school a few days apart, and the police are investigating both deaths in detail.

"We have a source that confirmed to us that the police are considering one of the medical students who was at the scene of the first murder as a potential suspect."

Zora didn't hear anything else as the walls began to close in on her. Her hands shook, and the remote clattered to the ground. Zora stumbled back onto the couch and gripped the armrest as her chest tightened. She smacked a hand against her rib cage as if to relieve the pressure and took quick deep breaths, in and out, in and out, until she could breathe more easily.

This was turning into a nightmare. She knew from Silas she was a potential suspect, but she hadn't expected some of the information had already leaked to the press, especially since the police had no evidence tying her to the murders. It was only a matter of time before the name of the suspected medical student—her name— was leaked. At that point, even if she was able to clear the suspicions against her, the damage would have been done to her reputation. No medical residency program would want to take a chance on her. And her dream, the one she'd worked hard for all these years, would go *poof*. Just like that.

Her chest began to tighten again—a sign of another impending panic attack—but Zora quelled it. She couldn't afford to become unhinged, and right now, she needed all her wits about her to clear her name.

Zora wasn't interested in turning the attention away from herself onto another innocent victim. So, the only course of action left was to identify the real killer. And Zora had to find him as soon as possible.

She knew just the right person for the job. She'd planned to call him before, but now she needed to do so ASAP.

Zora picked up her phone and dialed the number.

13

Z ora leaned back on the couch as the call connected to Marcus Tate. She'd first met Marcus just after her sister had disappeared. He was a spindly teen when her mother had rescued him from the juvenile justice system as part of her pro-bono work. Marcus had been charged with a truancy offense, but her mother had discerned he possessed a keen mind and was only bored with attending school. So her mother had hired him to work a few hours a week at her law firm.

Marcus had taken to investigating like a duck took to water and had ended up going back to school and graduating with a major in Criminology and Criminal Justice from the University of Maryland-College Park. He'd come back to work full-time for her mother after college and had risen quickly through the ranks to become one of the lead investigators. Over the years, Marcus had always acted like a big brother to Zora.

"Hi, Marcus," Zora said.

"Hey, little sis, how are you doing?" Marcus asked.

"I'm okay."

"What's up?"

"I need your help. And I need you to not tell my mother." Zora knew this was a hard ask given that Marcus worked for her mother, but the last thing she wanted was her mother butting into her business. Her relationship with her mother was already tenuous at best, and she didn't need it to get any worse, which was what typically happened when her mother got involved.

There was silence on the line, and Zora held her breath as she waited.

"Okay," Marcus finally said. "How can I help?"

Zora let out a sigh of relief. She told him all that had happened from when she'd found the dead body until discovering she was a suspect for the two cases. She could hear him tapping his pen against his desk as he listened. Zora knew Marcus well enough to know he only did that when he was upset.

"I need to find out who the real killer is," Zora said. "And the best place to start is to find out more about the victims. A background check on them would be very helpful to see if they're connected in anyway," she finished.

"I can do that. But are you okay? This must be very stressful."

Zora felt the tears sting her eyes and fought the urge to break down and sob. With Marcus, she could always be herself. But right now, she needed to hold back and not lose it, which was what would happen if she started crying. "I'm upset and mad and frightened all at the same time. Everything feels like a dream, like it's happening to someone else."

"Hang in there, little sis. We're not going to let anything happen to you."

Even though Zora had known Marcus was always on her side, it was nice to hear the affirmation.

"But Zora, you know this could become very dangerous."

Of course, Zora was definitely scared. Who wouldn't be? Whoever was at the bottom of this had already proven they were willing to take multiple lives. But Zora wasn't going to let anyone cut short her life and her dreams without a fight.

She fiddled with her pendant. "I know," she said.

"But what else can I do? I need to find out the truth. That's the only way I can be set free from this suspicion. You know my career means everything to me. If it gets derailed, I don't know what I'd do. And I could even lose my life if I'm charged and convicted."

"I still think you should let your mom know. This is her wheelhouse."

Zora sat up. "No way. I need people who would truly give their best to help me. People I can easily get in touch with. People I can trust with my life. My mother isn't one of them. I'm not sure my heart can take it if she stands me up for yet another one of her meetings when I really need her. It would be the final straw."

"Okay, okay. No need to get all worked up. I'll get on it ASAP and get back to you. We'll beat this, okay? You know I'm here for you if you ever need to chat."

"Yes, I know. Thanks again, Marcus. I'll talk to you later." Zora ended the call.

Marcus. Zora wasn't surprised Marcus hadn't asked her to take her hands off the case. He knew enough about her to know that would be futile.

Her shoulders relaxed. It felt good to have him in her corner. Zora could always rely on him—Marcus had been there for her any time she needed his help over the years.

A smile tugged at the corner of her lips, and her face grew warm as she remembered having a crush on him when she was younger and acting like a lovesick puppy around him. She still liked him now, but only as a brother.

Then her smile waned as she remembered what she was up against. Possible murder charges against her and a mark on her record, damage to her reputation, loss of the opportunity to get a good placement to train as a surgeon, and possible loss of her freedom.

Zora sighed and closed her eyes. She'd set the ball rolling. Now, she needed to focus on her next step: finding out more about the killer. The best place to start was at the crime scenes. The Gross Anatomy lab had been closed off, so no access there. But there was no guarantee it was the primary crime scene— Zora hadn't noticed any other disturbed areas in the lab that morning. The killer could have murdered Martha Adams somewhere else and transported her to the lab.

She would visit the parking lot instead, the place where Professor Oakley died. It might not be the primary crime scene as well, but it was more likely he'd been killed there. Going there tomorrow night might be the best option since the place was probably buzzing with police officers tonight. Zora didn't see the point in giving the cops something else against her if she was caught snooping. And she wouldn't have the freedom to search the area as she would have liked if she went there tonight, but she expected the police to be all done and packed up by tomorrow.

Besides, even if by some miracle the police were all gone by now, her body ached all over. She could easily miss something important in her exhaustion if she went there now. And she was still reeling from what had happened at the station earlier today.

Yes, tomorrow was definitely better. By then, she would be rested and alert.

And maybe she would find something the police missed.

14

Drake stifled a yawn as he stretched with his legs spread apart and his arms above his head. He stood in front of the fifteen-foot floor-to-ceiling windows in his bachelor penthouse and absorbed the sun rays that lit up the room and magnified the opulence of the eight-thousand-square-foot suite. He'd just finished his regular early morning swim in the infinity pool on the private rooftop terrace and had taken a quick shower afterwards in his marble master bath. Drake was refreshed, energized, and pleased with how well the last two nights had gone. It was good to be young and alive.

His lips tugged up at the corners just thinking

about her. Susie had been special—the rumors about her had been right. She'd met his demands and then some. In fact, she'd totally drained his energy, the first ever to do so. There had been lots of girls and women in his life, but Susie topped them all. He was so pleased with her he'd made arrangements with the club to make sure she was available to him whenever he called. The H Club had acquiesced to his request. They'd had to—a lot of money had changed hands.

Drake let out another big yawn and padded back on his warmed feet to the massive beige lounge that took up the bulk of the living room space. It was time to get ready for the day, since he had business to take care of, even though it was the weekend. He didn't believe in going to church or all that nonsense his father tried to push on him. Church was for poor and desperate people as far as he was concerned. Drake was neither. He would start with his morning paper and then eat the breakfast that Tiny had prepared.

He picked up the Sunday paper from the coffee table and reclined on the lounge. The news of Professor Oakley's death dominated the headlines and stared back at him. He remembered the guy, tall and pompous with a superior attitude. But Drake had been able to drive fear into him. As usual, he'd had a weakness Drake had been able to exploit. If the professor was dead, it was probably his own fault. Only the strong survived.

Drake glossed over the rest of the page with disinterest. Murder was nothing new, and people died every day. He was about to flip over the front page, when a small section in the far left column caught his eye. The reporter stated that sources from the police indicated that Professor Oakley was likely the killer's second victim, with Martha Adams as the first.

He felt a tiny alarm ring in his head. Maybe it was a coincidence, and his thoughts were mistaken. But Drake hadn't survived this long in the business by ignoring his warning instincts. Somehow, he couldn't dismiss the thought that something was wrong. He rapped his knuckles on the coffee table.

Tiny appeared at his side, his muscular build clad in black workout clothes, and his bald head shining with sweat.

Drake jabbed at the front page of the newspaper. "I need you to find out more about these cases," he said.

Tiny nodded in assent and left. He was a man of few words.

Drake flipped the front page and continued reading the rest of the paper.

There was no point in dwelling on the matter until he had all the information he'd asked for.

Tiny would make sure he got everything he needed to know.

15

I n the hovel he called an apartment, the man searched the pockets of the work uniforms in his closet for the pin he always carried. Each one came up empty. He couldn't find the pin. It was his good luck charm—it calmed him and gave him the courage he needed to take care of what had to be done. He leaned his head against the door of the closet and tried to recall when he'd last seen it.

He remembered holding it in his fingers and rubbing it while waiting in the back seat for the professor to arrive. The killings, though necessary, didn't come easy, and the pin helped him get in the zone. He couldn't recall if he'd put it back into his pocket.

The man had always been careful about not

leaving any evidence behind, using latex gloves, a hair net over his grey-streaked hair, a mask over his long gaunt face, and the hooded jacket. But he hadn't expected the professor to fight him so hard, which was probably how the pin had dropped. He'd put up a good struggle, but the professor was no match for him, and the man had been able to subdue him and inject the noxious fluid into his veins. He'd then positioned him on the steering wheel so anyone seeing him would assume he was asleep. The man had planned to bring him back to the lab, but leaving him in the car had seemed like a better idea and less risky, since he couldn't afford to get caught until everything was over.

The man shuffled over to his bedside table and picked up the picture frame sitting on it. The face that stared back at him was smiling, her beautiful blonde hair in wisps around her face, and her pale blue eyes shining with joy. He missed her greatly. It was all his fault since he hadn't been able to protect her. He hadn't noticed the warning signs, and by the time he did, she was already dead.

Life without her had become meaningless. She'd loved to laugh and had teased him all the time. She'd never complained about the small home they'd lived in— the old rickety furniture and faded curtains, the leaking bathroom with its constant dripping no matter how many times the plumbers looked at it, the tiny room her bed barely fit in, the constant pungent smell from the open sewers around their building, and the heat turned off by the landlord at night. Instead, she'd tried all she could to make it a place worth coming home to. They'd been poor, but she'd treated everything he'd ever bought her like a treasure to be savored.

She hadn't only been the light of his life but of others as well. She was always bringing strays home, both human and animal. And she would share whatever she had with them. His thin lips curled upwards at the thought. He'd complained at the time, but now he would have been willing to accept as many strays as she wanted if only it would bring her back.

He placed the picture frame back on the bedside table and noticed a colorful brochure sticking out from under the books piled on the other end of it. He picked it up. It was a travel brochure for Bali, the place they'd both dreamed of traveling to and vacationing in. He held it close to his nose. He could still smell the baby's breath scent, the smell she loved to wear. Baby's breaths had been her favorite flower.

The man's stomach twisted. He still wished she was here. He could remember how excited she'd been whenever they'd talked about the trip. She'd kept a list of hundred and one things to accomplish there. She had wanted to go after college graduation before she got married, but he'd insisted they wait until he retired. Now they would never go. Another dream destroyed.

He balled his fist and crushed the brochure in his hand. He would never forgive the monster who'd snuffed out her light and crushed her like a bug under his feet. And the others who'd helped him drive the nail into her heart.

The man felt rage boiling up within him. They would pay, every last one of them. He would make them regret what they'd done. A life for a life—none would go scot free. The next stage of his plan was already in motion.

But first he needed to find the pin—it had been a gift from her.

It wasn't in the hands of the cops or they would have come looking for him, since they were anxious to close the cases and would pursue every lead. And he would have known.

That could only mean one thing: the pin was likely back at the crime scene.

The man made his decision.

16

Zora parked her car a few spots away from the yellow tape cordoning off the area and headed to the crime scene. The professor's car, which she'd seen on the TV news broadcast, had been taken away. All that remained was a white outline on the oil-stained concrete floor marking the spot where the car had been parked. The smell of gasoline hung thick in the air.

She looked around the parking garage, and nothing else seemed amiss. But bright lights now illuminated the section that was undergoing renovations. Zora had been in this parking lot before at night when she'd taken Genetics classes in the building, and this area of the garage had always had an eerie feel to it.

It seemed the murder had forced the school to finally change the lighting.

Zora moved closer to the cars packed near the crime scene tape. There was a white BMW on the left with barely any dust on the body. The car must have been parked recently, so she dismissed the thought of finding anything important there.

She made her way to the right side of the cordoned area. There was a red Ford pickup truck parked there with a thick undisturbed dust coating on its cracked windshield and flattish worn tires already showing their threads. If there were any clues to be found, this would be the spot.

Zora inspected the exterior of the car but found nothing. Careful not to disturb the dust layers, she bent down and looked under the cab. She didn't see anything and was about to get up when she spotted a reflective glint off a small object.

She grabbed a Kleenex tissue from her pocket and extended her hand into the area where she'd seen the sparkle. She picked up the object carefully, and when she pulled her hand out, she discovered it was a small round pin with an American eagle head and a worn Vietnam war veteran insignia on it. It looked clean with barely any dust on it, which meant it had only been there recently.

Zora lifted the pin closer to her nose and sniffed. The faint noxious smell of formaldehyde mixed with what she could tell was baby's breath hit her nostrils. She was familiar with the flora from her love for coffee—Zora had drunk many flora-inspired lattes which was all the rage now in trendy coffee shops. Formaldehyde, on the other hand, was not a common scent found anywhere, only typically among those who handled embalmed dead bodies or body parts. Or a killer who worked with formalin.

She felt adrenaline rush through her. Maybe this was it, what she was hoping to find. She wrapped the tissue carefully around the pin and tucked it into her pocket. She would examine it in detail later.

A further search of the area yielded nothing else, so she decided it was time to head back home.

When Zora reached her car, there was a note on her windshield held in place by the wiper. It hadn't been there before. She picked up the note, opened it, and read the four words written on it:

LEAVE THE CASE ALONE.

Even though her heart raced, Zora looked around the parking lot but didn't see anyone. Who'd placed the note on her car? The killer? How had the killer known she'd be here?

As she studied the note, she heard the faint

sounds of a heavy door closing. Her head snapped in the direction of the sound, and she saw the door leading up the stairwell swing shut.

Zora dropped the note into her pocket and took off running. Her guess was that whoever had gone through that door was the person who'd dropped the note.

She pulled the door open and rushed in. She'd never taken exercise seriously, and it soon showed in her heavy breathing. She looked up the stairwell to see a man of lean build in a hooded jacket scurrying up the stairs two floors above. Though the man seemed stooped, he moved with unexpected agility.

Zora raced up the stairwell after him with all her strength, huffing and puffing all the way. But the man was far ahead, and she couldn't catch up. By the time she got to the final floor where she'd last seen him, the door leading into the building's interior was locked. The door had a white sign at the top marked "Employees Only" in black, and a card reader on the side blinked a red light.

She pulled her student ID card from her jeans pocket and swiped it through the reader. The red light didn't turn green. Zora yanked the door handle, but the door stayed shut. She tried again with no result. Did this mean the killer was an employee?

There was no way to continue following the man, so Zora trudged down the stairs and made her way to her car.

It was time to go home. At least she had the pin with her.

Maybe it would yield some clues about the killer's identity.

———————

Now back at home, Zora picked up the pin using forceps from a pack of medical tools her mother had given her as a gift when she'd gained admission into medical school. She'd never thought she'd need it before her clinical years, but it had come in handy today.

The lamp on her desk cast a yellow glow on the pin as she sat at her desk and studied it. The surface of the pin appeared worn smooth. Maybe the owner had rubbed its surface multiple times, which meant there was a high probability the owner's DNA was on it.

Zora's pulse quickened. Maybe this was the break they were looking for. She'd called Marcus as soon as she'd gotten home to tell him what she'd found, and he'd promised to be at her home in the next twenty minutes.

She checked her watch. He should have arrived by now.

The doorbell rang. As Zora got up and made her way to the front door, she could still feel the aches in her legs from the sprinting she'd done. Her body was probably out of shape, but Zora hated working out— she'd broken the New Year's resolutions far too many times.

She reached the door and looked through the peephole. Sure enough, Marcus was standing outside, looking very much at ease.

Zora turned the lock and slid the bolt before removing the chain latch and opening the door. Marcus stood tall, dressed in blue jeans and a white polo shirt with custom stitching on the front breast pocket that brought out the grey in his eyes. He had a small satchel slung over his shoulder. Seeing him looking so good reminded her of why she'd had a crush on him before.

Zora stepped aside to let him in. "Thanks for coming over."

"No worries," he responded.

"Do you need a drink?" Zora asked as she walked into the kitchen.

Marcus sat on one of the kitchen bar stools and dropped his satchel on the countertop. "Yes. Water is fine." He looked around the living room. "Your apartment looks nice."

"Thank you," Zora said. "I guess it's your first time here since I moved in." She grabbed a bottle of water from the fridge and a glass from the cupboard and poured a glass of water for him.

Zora could feel Marcus' eyes on her. "I don't recall ever being invited to a housewarming party," he said as she placed the glass in front of him.

"I didn't have one. I barely moved in before classes started, so I nuked the idea."

Marcus lifted the glass and took a sip. Zora watched him drink and marveled at how gorgeous he looked even as his Adam's apple bobbed.

Once he was done, he set the glass back down on the countertop. "Okay, let's get down to business. Can I see the pin?"

"Give me one second." Zora walked into her room, returned with the tissue, and moved instead to the coffee table in the living room. There she opened up the tissue on its surface to expose the pin. She wanted no chance of water getting on it.

Marcus rose from the kitchen stool and joined her beside the coffee table. He stooped down and stared at the pin. "This is an interesting one. It looks like something made for veterans."

He took the forceps from Zora and turned it. "There is a tiny set of numbers here on the back. I think we can use that to track down the owner." He placed the pin back on the tissue and sat on his hunches.

"That would be great," Zora said.

Marcus cast a stern look at her, and Zora braced herself for the lecture she was about to receive.

"Zora, what were you doing going to the crime scene?" Marcus said, his steely grey eyes leveled at her. "What if the police had seen you? You could have been suspected of tampering with evidence!"

Zora bristled. This was her life they were talking about. She didn't understand how anyone expected her to sit still and do nothing. "Well, they didn't see me. I couldn't just sit back and watch while my whole life went down the toilet," she said, the sparks in her eyes matching his.

Marcus rubbed his hand across his brow. "I'm just worried about you," he said gently. "What if your life becomes endangered from your getting involved? What if the killer was there?"

Zora said nothing. She averted her eyes and rubbed the back of her neck.

Marcus narrowed his eyes. "Wait. What aren't you telling me?"

"It's not a big deal."

"I'll decide that," he insisted.

So Zora told him about the note and the man in the hooded jacket.

Marcus blew out his breath and ran his fingers through his hair. "Darn it, Zora! That's it. You have to leave the investigation alone. Where is the note?"

Zora pulled the note gingerly from her pocket and placed it on the coffee table. She grabbed the forceps from Marcus and spread the note apart with it.

Marcus read the note and said nothing. He got up, strode back to the kitchen countertop, and pulled two small evidence bags from his satchel. He walked back to the coffee table and took the forceps from Zora, then bent down and used the forceps to put the pin and the note into the evidence bags. "I have a friend in forensics who owes me a favor. I'll give these items to him to analyze." Marcus straightened up. "Maybe we might be able to get something from them or not."

"Do you think he'll be able to get back to you quickly?"

"He should." He walked back to the kitchen and put the evidence bags into his satchel and slung the bag over his shoulder. "I have to leave now so I can get this to him as soon as possible."

"Isn't it too late in the day?"

Marcus shook his head. "He's always at the lab. It's practically his home."

He walked toward the door and then turned. Zora was following closely behind and almost bumped into him.

"I mean it, Zora. No more investigating. Please. It's too dangerous. Silas and I will help you get out of this mess, okay? I'll let you know once I hear back from my friend," he said.

"What about the link between the victims? Have you found anything?"

"I haven't discovered any connections so far, but I'll keep digging."

"What about Silas? I haven't heard back from him."

"He's out of town for a case, but I know he hasn't been able to get the name of the witness. That Detective Morris is really holding it close to his chest. I'm sure we'll hit pay dirt soon. But you have to stay safe until then, okay?"

Zora nodded in assent.

Marcus gave a quick wave and was gone.

She closed the door and leaned against it in relief.

Zora had presented a bold front to Marcus, but to be honest, the note had scared her.

But she was running out of time, and her life was on the line. Any moment now, her name would leak to the press.

Contrary to what Marcus thought, she couldn't sit back and twiddle her thumbs.

She had to save herself.

So she was going to continue investigating until she exposed the truth.

17

The man entered his apartment, removed his hooded jacket, and stuffed it behind his clothes at the back of his closet. He would burn it later. He had so many it wouldn't be missed.

A hacking cough racked through his body, exacerbated by the strong smell of garlic from his neighbors, and his lungs fought his desire to breathe in.

The man pulled his handkerchief from his jeans pockets and coughed into it. Once the coughing stopped, he examined the handkerchief and found it tinged with blood. He didn't react at the sight, but instead stuffed the cloth back into his pocket and then walked over to the windows to close them.

His mind went back to the parking garage as he secured the window handles.

Zora Smyth had almost caught him.

He'd been surprised to see her snooping around the garage. She definitely had gumption—the possibility of police presence hadn't kept her away. She would have had a lot of explaining to do if she'd been caught.

Not that he cared. Especially since she reminded him of someone. A person he hated. It would have worked out perfectly for him if the police had caught her. That way they would close the case and never bother to find him. He, on the other hand, had a legitimate excuse for being in the area. But she would have remembered who he was if she'd seen him, and that was something he couldn't afford right now.

The man had seen her pick something from the floor, but he wasn't sure if it was the pin. And there was no way to find out. As much as he hated to lose the pin, it wasn't a priority for him. His desire for revenge ranked higher on the scale, and searching for the pin could put it at risk. If they ever traced it to him, he could always claim he'd lost it there, and no one would bat an eyelid at his excuse, since he had a legitimate reason for being in that parking lot.

He rubbed his hands together and blew a warm breath into them. The apartment was freezing as expected. The nights were getting colder, and the cold tended to slow him down, causing a deep ache in his bones. Even his sleep had gotten worse.

The man searched his closet for his red sweater and pulled it on. The ugly sweater had been a silly Christmas gift from her, and he'd hardly worn it while she was alive. Now, he liked to wear it often— it made him feel closer to her.

His loved one.

The man's heart hurt just thinking about her. He tried to dwell only on how she'd always looked, but all he could see was how she'd been at the end, her body bent like a rag doll.

His vision clouded, and he ground his clenched teeth. Those who had hurt her needed to be punished.

There was no way he would stop now.

No, there would be no mercy for them until he was done.

18

Drake looked down at the file in front of him. Tiny had done a good job of pulling together all the information he could find on the two cases.

His contact at the police station had been very helpful. Well, he'd had no choice, since a significant amount of Drake's money flowed into his pockets.

Drake began to review the reports again. Even though the victims had died in what seemed to be two different circumstances, both victims had been injected with formalin. Their blood results had also yielded a high level of Rohypnol, yet there was no evidence of sexual assault in either case. It was unusual to use both formalin and Rohypnol as the weapons of choice in the deaths, and Drake wondered what message the killer was trying to send.

He continued scanning the information in front of him. The police suspected the killer must have been a relatively young man given the strength needed to subdue both victims—someone who most likely worked out in one form or the other. There was also evidence of a struggle in both cases, but no DNA or prints had been left behind. The killer had been careful.

Drake could also see that a medical student had been identified as a potential suspect in the case. Zora Smyth was her name, according to the reports. He looked at the attached photo. She was pretty with guileless eyes that drew him in. Something about her reminded him of someone he knew, but he couldn't place who it was. Drake felt a stirring within himself as he continued to gaze at the picture, a magnetism that drew him to her.

He shut down any further thoughts about her and closed the file. Drake had promised himself that he would never lose control again. Not while the company was at stake.

Drake opened the drawer on the right to place the file in it but changed his mind. Instead, he flipped through the reports again and extracted Zora Smyth's picture before placing the file in the drawer. The picture, he tucked into his wallet. He would keep it with him in the meantime.

He rested his elbows on his desk and steepled his fingers. So far, it seemed the police didn't have a lot to go on. There was also not enough information in the reports to confirm his personal theory.

Drake pressed the hidden button on his desk. A moment later, Tiny stepped into his office, wearing black pants and a black button-down shirt rolled up at the sleeves.

"I need you to keep an eye on these cases and let me know once there are any updates," Drake said.

"Yes, sir," Tiny replied.

"Did you check into the man like I requested?"

"Yes, I did. He's still working at the same place. He looks much frailer now, but there's no evidence that he works out—I had him followed, and so far I've found nothing out of the ordinary. But I've asked some guys to keep an eye on him."

"Okay, keep digging into the people around him to see if there is any person of interest. I'm not yet convinced these cases are related to us, but I'm not going to take any chances."

"I'll let you know if I learn anything new," Tiny replied.

Drake dismissed him with a wave of his hand. Tiny would do his job, but Drake needed to keep an eye on the case as well. The niggling doubt at the back of his mind was still there, and Drake had learned to trust his instincts.

He was sure he would find something of importance sooner or later.

19

Zora sat across Marcus in the local gourmet coffee shop. It was two blocks away from her apartment and served specialty coffee from various far-flung places around the world. Zora loved to come here when she didn't have time to make her own coffee. She enjoyed its cool ambience —the simple mint green and chocolate brown decor, the smell of freshly ground coffee mixed with fresh homemade bread, the large windows that filled the space with natural light, and the comfortable chairs set in nooks. Zora sat in one such nook this morning.

Luckily, she had no scheduled classes today. The school gave the students a day off each month, and today was that free day. It was just as well since the Martha Adams case consumed Zora's every waking thought, making it hard for her to focus on anything else. She'd been relieved when Marcus had called and asked her to meet him here. He must have come into new information about the case.

Zora picked her cup of coffee and inhaled deeply. The sweet jasmine and peach floral notes from the Ethiopian Guji coffee wafted up her nostrils. She took a sip and the tea-like liquid filled her taste buds and warmed her body. Guji coffee was not her favorite, but it was a close second. Zora took another sip and then felt Marcus' eyes on her.

"I could watch you enjoy your coffee all day," he said, his voice low and soothing.

Zora felt a smile tug at the corners of her lips. "I can't help it. It's one of my favorite things in the world." The aroma of good coffee always calmed her. Now more than ever, she needed to hold onto this piece of happiness even as her world turned upside down.

The smile left her face as she remembered why she was here. Zora set the cup of coffee on the table and leaned back on the chair. "What do you have for me?" she asked.

Marcus pulled his notes from his satchel and scanned through. "I didn't find anything fishy in Martha Adams' background. She was single, lived alone, and worked at the Collmark group as a Senior HR Manager after being promoted a year ago. She was last seen leaving her office building before she ended up on your dissection table. Even though she wasn't the most popular at work, she didn't seem to have any enemies.

"Professor Oakley, on the other hand, seemed to have had some issues with money. He had a specific amount leave his account every month, and we traced it to a group involved in racketeering and blackmail. So it's safe to assume he was being blackmailed before he died."

Zora leaned forward and put her elbows on the table. "Any ideas on what he was being blackmailed for?"

"I haven't found anything yet, but I'm sure I will soon," Marcus said. He took a sip of his own coffee and grimaced. Marcus wasn't really a coffee drinker.

He also had dark circles under his bloodshot eyes. "You look exhausted," she said. It was her fault—she'd done this to him.

Marcus gave her a small smile. "It's nothing," he said and then flipped through his notes. "The bad news is I didn't find any connections between Professor Oakley and Martha Adams."

Zora slumped in her chair and tried to hide her

disappointment. She took another sip of coffee and grimaced as she swallowed. The coffee now tasted ashy in her mouth.

"Don't worry, Zora," Marcus said. "I'll keep checking to see if something pops up. I have some good news though." His gorgeous grey eyes shone with excitement. "I got the forensic results back from my friend regarding the pin," he said. "He didn't find any DNA on it. However, each pin was sold to an actual veteran, and my friend was able to use the number imprinted on the pin to track down the buyer."

Zora sat at the edge of her chair. "Who was it?"

Marcus looked at his notes. "His name is Danny Thompson, and he's a security guard for the Coll-mark group."

"Bingo!" Zora almost jumped up from her seat. "Martha Adams worked at the same company. So it's likely that this case might have something to do with the Collmark group." She beamed at Marcus. "Awe-some work."

"Thank you." Marcus closed his notes and leaned forward. "But Zora, I think we should turn this infor-mation over to the cops and let them take it from here. I don't want you doing anything that might put you in danger. Two people have already died, and I'd rather keep you off that list."

Zora fingered her pendant. "Okay, I'll back off a little, but I'm still going to keep an eye on how things are going."

Marcus sighed. "I can't convince you otherwise, can I?"

Zora gave a tentative smile and said nothing.

"I'll meet with the detectives later today and tell them everything," Marcus said. "Promise me you'll call me before you do anything."

"I will." Zora reached across and patted his hand. "Don't worry."

"Why is it that I'm *worried* when I hear that?"

Zora chuckled. "Relax, I won't give you any premature grey hairs."

Marcus gave her a disbelieving look, and Zora chuckled again.

He packed his notes into his satchel. "I wish I could stay, but I have to return to the office before your mom starts looking for me."

Zora's spine stiffened. "She has you on a short leash, doesn't she?" she said.

Marcus gave her a piercing glance and said nothing. He was used to the strained relationship between

Zora and her mother. He got up and slung his satchel on his shoulder. Zora rose as well.

"I'll see you later," Marcus said. "Stay safe, okay?" Zora nodded. He gave her a quick side hug and strode out of the coffee shop.

Zora sat down again and leaned back in the chair. The Collmark group. She'd read about them briefly while browsing a news article online.

It was an investment firm that had forced the management of a biotech company to trigger a "poison pill" strategy to prevent a hostile takeover. The biotech management had offered a preferred stock option to its shareholders, allowing them to exercise their purchase rights at a huge premium to the company, which made the cost of the takeover prohibitive. Collmark group had been forced to back down.

She knew little else about the company. Maybe Silas might know more, since he had deep roots in this town. But he was away on a client's case today, so she resolved to ask him tomorrow when he got back.

Zora pulled out her phone and clicked open the search engine. *Collmark group ... let's see what else I can dig up about you.*

20

Tonight had been a great night for Calvin. He'd finally bagged the deal, earning enormous profits for the company, while manipulating the other party to leave key deal terms on the table. They still didn't know what had hit them. That was what Calvin was really good at. He wondered what would happen once they realized what they'd lost.

Calvin laughed. He'd become the envy of his colleagues. Tom had congratulated him. Sarah had been elated, especially since she would now end up with a larger office space. He also trusted her to spread the news through the office grapevine.

He inhaled deeply. The smell of money was in the air, and Calvin could already see lots of it—his bonus

—pouring into his account. He already had plans for the funds. It was time to achieve his long-time dream.

The H Club.

The doors of the exclusive club were now open to him. It was rumored the club looked both at the depth of a prospective member's pockets as well as their influence in Lexinbridge society. Calvin didn't know what specific criteria they measured these two factors against, but he was certain he'd earned his way in.

Though the news of the deal would hit the financial community before sundown, H Club would have heard about it by now—they certainly had their finger on the pulse of everything, and Calvin expected an invitation from the club soon. He now had the chance to be connected to Lexinbridge's elite, the folks whose word was law in the town. Calvin's star could only rise higher from there. He imagined all the women that would flock to his side once he joined. It was a great day indeed.

Calvin had been so elated he'd already treated himself to a special bottle of 1970 Napoleon, which he kept hidden in one of his desk drawers. One shot had turned into two, and then three, until he couldn't drive himself home. So he called for car service.

Once the building security informed him his car service was waiting up front, Calvin grabbed his briefcase and left the office, his thoughts on how much his life had changed. He'd been a senior associate at Beckett & Schubert years ago, where his chances of making it to the top had been slim. There'd been too many cutthroat associates just like him and only one partnership slot. Calvin had done the math, so when an opportunity opened up a year ago to move in as in-house counsel for the Collmark group—where he didn't have to work as hard to make the same amount of money—he jumped ship, terrible affair aside. Now his decision was paying off, and in big chunks. Yes, he was loving his life right now.

Calvin swayed on his feet as he pressed the button to call the elevator. He could hardly see straight, but he didn't care. This was his night to cele-brate, and nothing could stop him from doing so. Though he was sure most employees had left by now, he convinced himself he could still walk straight if he encountered anyone he knew.

But right now, all Calvin wanted was to go home and rest. It had been a long day. He'd have more time to celebrate tomorrow. And maybe the H Club would have sent him an invitation by then. His face split into a grin just thinking about it.

The elevator pinged, and the doors opened. It was

already occupied—Drake Pierce, a vice president in the company, stood at the back of the elevator with his bodyguard by his side.

Calvin knew who Drake was—someone no one wanted to cross. Drake was ruthless and practically had the board of directors in his pocket. Everyone knew the old man's influence was waning, and that Drake was really the person in control, his bodyguard always by his side.

He shivered. The bodyguard gave Calvin the creeps. He'd met him face-to-face once before, and he hadn't liked him then. But it'd been necessary at the time. He could imagine the guy crushing people with his large meaty hands. The long, jagged scar on his face did not help in lightening its ferocity.

Calvin stepped into the elevator and greeted Drake, who barely acknowledged him. One would think they hadn't met before from the disinterested way the guy looked at him. Calvin faced the elevator doors as they closed, and the elevator moved downward. He held his black briefcase in front of his body and only looked ahead, using all his efforts to keep still and not reveal how drunk he was.

He could feel eyes boring into him from behind, and his back twitched. Calvin couldn't tell if it was Drake or the bodyguard staring at him, but he resolved not to allow their rudeness to affect his mood tonight. After all, if all went well, he and Drake could wind up as members of the same club. And since he wasn't sure how much influence Drake had on who joined, there was no need to get on his bad side.

The elevator pinged as it reached the ground floor, and the doors slid open. Calvin stepped out of the elevator and walked stiffly across the lobby without looking back. He gave a nod to the security guard who was on duty and stepped out into the open air.

He took a deep breath. The air was breezy, its scent tinged with the sweet-smelling aroma of victory and success. Now he could relax.

Calvin saw the black town car idling in front of the building entrance. It was the only one there, so he assumed it must be his car. He opened the rear door and slipped in, placing his black briefcase beside him on the back seat. The driver was clad as usual in a black suit but was also wearing a set of black sunglasses. Calvin didn't recognize him, but that didn't matter. The car service could have hired more employees.

The driver greeted him with a gravelly voice, and Calvin nodded. He wasn't interested in making small talk. He just needed the driver to get him home safely.

Calvin leaned back on the plush black leather seats and closed his eyes as the car moved forward. He didn't know when he drifted off to sleep.

He woke up when he felt the car roll to a stop. As Calvin struggled to come fully awake, he felt a stab in his thigh and looked up to see a man in a black mask staring back at him from the driver's seat.

Calvin yelped, and fear gripped his heart. He didn't know who the man was, but he wasn't going to wait around and find out. He grabbed the door handle and tried to push it open, but the door on his side was locked. Calvin banged against the door, and when that didn't work, he picked up his briefcase and smashed the car window. But he didn't even make a dent.

As his limbs grew weak, Calvin took a deep breath, lifted his briefcase with difficulty, and put all his power behind it to try again. The glass shattered on the second attempt.

He stuck his hand through the glass and opened the door from the outside. The broken glass nicked his skin and blood ran down his forearm, but Calvin didn't care. Saving his life was more important.

Then the door swung open, and Calvin fell out. The man in the mask made no attempt to stop him.

Calvin could barely move his body, and the blades of grass scratched his skin with each crawl he attempted. His eyes darted around in fright, and he saw he was in the middle of a field of wide flowers interspersed with long blades of grass. There were no buildings around, and the field seemed void of any other human presence.

Soon Calvin found it hard to breathe. His vision became hazy, and somehow, he knew his end had come. This was it—he would not live to see tomorrow. The H Club would forever remain a pipe dream.

With rage in his heart and regret in his bones, the man in the mask was the last person Calvin saw standing in front of him before his world collapsed.

21

*Z*ora adjusted her book bag on her shoulder as she stepped out of the lecture hall into the hallway. The air buzzed with chatter as students clad mostly in jeans and T-shirts strode in all directions to various sections of the building. She'd just finished her second lecture of the day, and it had ended fifteen minutes early. Classes had resumed despite the incidents at the school, but Zora hadn't been able to concentrate on what the professors were teaching. Her mind had been preoccupied with the Collmark group.

She hadn't learned anything new about the company. There was very little information on their website, and a search through the online news articles had yielded nothing. Even the previous articles Zora had read about them some time ago could no longer be found on the internet. She assumed the Collmark group must have had them pulled.

Zora could hit the public library in town to see if they had old news articles on file, but her morning was packed. And she had a Practice of Medicine— POM— session all afternoon. The library would be closed by the time she was done for the day.

Her phone buzzed. Zora retrieved it from her pants, checked the screen, and saw the notification that she'd received an email from the student financial services office. She unlocked her screen and opened the email. Zora hadn't been awarded the school scholarship she'd applied for.

She stiffened. What had happened? She'd already gotten unofficial confirmation from the staff that the scholarship was hers. What could have gone wrong?

Zora looked at the time on her phone. She had thirteen minutes before her lab started. If she hurried, she could get to the financial office and return with time to spare.

She raced down the hallway, sped through the walkway and soon arrived at the building floor that housed the financial office. Zora swung the double doors open and stepped in.

The student financial services office was filled

with cubicles, most of which where occupied by assistants either typing furiously into a computer or answering the phone. Zora headed to the nearest available assistant, whom she recognized.

"Hi, Stephanie," she said. "I'd like to speak with Ms. Wadsworth."

The assistant, Stephanie, looked up and gave Zora a weak smile. "Hi, Zora, Ms. Wadsworth is not in. Is there any way I can help you?" Her eyes flickered past Zora.

Zora followed her line of sight and noticed some of the other assistants had raised their heads and were staring at her. She turned back to Stephanie. "I just got the email that I didn't get the Stanton scholarship. I thought I was already selected for it."

"Zora, unfortunately, the scholarship committee chose a different candidate. Thomas Strickland."

"But—"

Stephanie got up. "Walk with me," she said quietly. "Come on." She grabbed a file from her cubicle and led the way out of the office. Zora followed her.

Once they were out through the doors, Stephanie turned to her. "Zora, you didn't hear this from me, but the committee had an urgent meeting this morning and dropped you."

Zora's eyes searched her face. "Why?"

Stephanie inventoried her surroundings and then looked back at Zora. "The rumors. They heard you were a suspect in the Martha Adams case. Someone sent an anonymous note to them. You know how reputation is everything here, so they met this morning and made a decision."

Zora staggered back. She'd been sentenced without a trial. *Who is it that's so intent on harming me? Why?*

"Are you okay?" Stephanie peered at her with concern.

"I'm good." Zora gave her a thin smile. "Thanks for telling me."

"Just so you know, I don't believe it one bit. But I have no say in the decisions."

"Thank you." Zora checked her phone and noticed she was running out of time. "I have to get back to class. I'll talk to you later."

"Take care, Zora. Everything will turn out alright."

Zora nodded and walked off. She felt Stephanie's eyes following her, but she straightened her shoulders, tipped her chin up, and held her book bag close to her body.

She would not cower since she'd done nothing to

be ashamed of. But how had the rumor spread through the school so fast, given the police had even withheld the information from the press?

Zora could fight the decision. She probably would have done that in the past. But there was a strong chance the scholarship committee wouldn't change their mind—they would just cite another reason for the rejection, and she'd have no way to disprove it. It might even make everything worse. And it wasn't like she really needed the money, even though the scholarship would have helped open doors in the medical world to her. Zora needed to pick her battles, and this one wasn't one of them.

She looked at her phone. She had seven minutes to get to the lab, so Zora hurried to the elevators, took one to the third floor, and then hurried back through the walkway. She checked her phone. Four minutes left.

Her shoulder brushed against someone. "Sorry," Zora said.

"You need to watch where you're going. Before you cause another disaster."

Zora turned to see Thomas Strickland. "What do you mean by that?"

"Don't be offended, Zora. In case you decide to murder me," he said in a mocking tone.

Zora stepped up to him. "What did you say?"

"We've all heard the rumors. How you killed that woman and even the professor. Did you hate him that much?"

Zora stared thoughtfully at Thomas. "It was you, wasn't it?"

Thomas swallowed. "I don't know what you're talking about."

Zora took another step toward him.

Thomas stumbled backward, shaking his head. "I didn't do anything!"

As if she'd believe him. "I'd be careful if I were you, especially if I did kill her. What would stop me from coming after you?"

Thomas' eyes widened. "You don't mean that."

Zora scoffed. "Would you like to bet on it?"

His face reddened as sweat broke out on his forehead. Then Thomas turned and fled.

Zora glared after him. She was sure he'd had a hand in the rumors, but there was no way to prove it.

She looked at her phone. *Shoot*. She was going to be late.

Zora sat on the kitchen bar stool in her apartment, eating an early dinner of a ham and pickle sandwich she'd picked up at the deli right outside campus on her way back from school.

After the encounter with Thomas Strickland, Zora had gone to the lab for her next class. But the atmosphere had been different. She'd noticed all the seats around her emptied as soon as she sat down. It was like she'd caught a plague, and no one wanted to be infected. Even those she considered her friends had averted their eyes and pretended not to know her. It had hurt. No one had bothered to ask her if the rumors were true. It had been the same way in the POM session.

Zora lifted her chin and pushed back her shoulders. Those people were not her true friends. Her real allies were on her side fighting with her. And she was going to find out the truth about these cases no matter what.

She took another bite of the sandwich. It now tasted like sawdust in her mouth, so she dumped the remainder in the garbage can. As Zora rinsed off her plate in the sink and dropped it in the dish rack, her phone rang. She turned off the tap, wiped her hands with the kitchen towel, and answered the phone.

"Hello, Silas," she said. "Welcome back."

"Thanks. How are you doing?" Silas asked. Zora could hear the sound of traffic in the background.

"I'm okay. So what do you have for me?" She leaned against the kitchen countertop as she waited for his response.

"The detectives found out about Danny Thompson and paid him a visit earlier today. Marcus told me about him."

"What did the guy say?"

"I heard from my source that he denied any knowledge of the murders and had strong alibis for where he was on the days the victims were murdered. CCTV footage confirmed his story. Hold on."

Zora heard some talking in the background and waited. She tapped the heel of her foot against the base of the kitchen island.

Soon Silas got back on the phone. "Zora, the police have just found a third victim, a lawyer—"

"Let me guess. He worked at the Collmark group?"

"Yes, for about a year," Silas replied in a surprised tone. "How did you know?"

Zora told him what Marcus had found out about the two victims. "He's already handed the information over to the police," she finished.

"Really? That means there has to be something

about the Collmark group that links them together. It can't be a coincidence that two victims and Danny Thompson work there, though it's not clear how the professor fits in."

"I'm still working on that angle," Zora said. "There must be a link there we just can't see right now." She turned and leaned her elbows on the countertop. "Hmmm. The plot thickens."

"I'm glad to see you make a joke. I've been so worried about how you're holding up."

"I'm keeping it together the best I can. Thanks for worrying about me."

"We just want you to stay safe," he said. "I'll follow up with the cops to see what else they've found."

"Do you know anything about the Collmark group?"

"I believe it's owned by John Pierce, a financier who made a killing during the internet boom. Since then, he's grown his company from a firm of five people to over two thousand employees. John Pierce is a businessman through and through and is always looking for the next company to take apart and sell in pieces. You don't want him getting his tentacles in your company. But the real nasty one is his son."

"His son?"

"Drake Pierce. He's very popular with the ladies. I've heard he likes to skirt around the law. If he sees a company he wants, he'll go after it like a mad dog and will do anything—I mean anything—to get it. But he's never been caught red-handed and has a team of lawyers to make sure that doesn't happen. There've even been some rumors that he's connected to the underworld. He's definitely someone you want to avoid."

"Gotcha."

"That's all I have for now. The cops plan to keep digging around Danny Thompson to see if there's anything. They think it's too coincidental that Danny Thompson and the lawyer worked at the Collmark group. That being said, the cops might just end up rattling the killer's cage with all their digging, so you need to be careful and stay safe."

"I will."

"Don't worry, Zora, we'll break this case. I'll call you if I hear anything else."

"Thanks for everything, Silas. I'll talk to you later." She ended the call and dropped her phone on the countertop.

Zora walked to the sink, grabbed a small spray bottle of water she kept close by, and made her way to the far corner of the living room, where she kept some indoor plants. Zora believed in infusing extra oxygen into the air if she could, and the plants were perfect for the job. She hadn't had a chance to water them for the past few days with all that had been going on, and the signs of neglect were beginning to show.

She thought about what she knew so far as she sprayed the plants. The first and the third victims were connected to the Collmark group. Since both the lawyer and HR manager were dead, it could mean it was related to an internal employee case, since HR staff dealt exclusively with employees. But how did the professor and now Danny Thompson fit in? Unless they were all connected in some other unknown way. But Zora didn't think that was the case. Her instincts were telling her she needed to dig deeper into the Collmark connection.

Zora finished spraying the plants and dropped the spray bottle back on the kitchen countertop. She picked her phone and dialed Marcus' number. He picked on the second ring.

"Hey, Marcus. I heard from Silas about Danny Thompson and his alibi," Zora said.

"Yeah. Sorry I didn't tell you as soon as I passed the information to the cops as we discussed. I just heard about their visit to him. Since we've been very helpful, I think it has slowed down their enthusiasm in charging you without evidence. But we're not out of the woods yet. Morris still seems super motivated. So what's up?"

Zora's anger flared at the mention of the detective's name. He seemed to have a very myopic view. Did he have something against women? Zora shelved that thought for now since she'd called Marcus for a reason.

"Silas just told me there's a third victim," she said. "He was an in-house counsel for Collmark, so I'm wondering if this has anything to do with an employee case. I was just thinking about it, and it seems Martha Adams was promoted a year ago and the lawyer got the job at Collmark a year ago as well. So what if this was about an employee case that happened around that time? Do you think you could dig into that? I know we might be chasing our tail here, but I have a feeling we're onto something."

"I'll see what I can do, though I can't promise anything," Marcus said. "HR data is typically hard to access. But I have a few ideas that might shake something loose."

"Thanks, Marcus. Anything you find could be helpful."

"Always my pleasure. Are you doing okay?"

"Yes, I am." Then he sighed. "You sound tired," Zora said.

"I am, and it's only afternoon. I still have a lot of work to take care of."

"Okay, I'll let you go. Talk to you soon."

"Later," Marcus said. Then Zora ended the call.

Her heart leaped with excitement as she leaned against the kitchen countertop. Zora had a feeling she was on the right track.

And maybe, just maybe, they'd be able to crack the case wide open before time ran out.

22

T he man finished his work for the day. It was a routine he was used to, and it hardly changed from day to day. He could perform the job with his eyes closed. He'd thought about leaving the job many years earlier, but had found that the positives of staying outweighed the negatives. And before he knew it, twenty years on the job had come and gone.

He would have to leave the job soon, once everything was over. Not that he'd miss it. It wasn't what he'd wanted to do with his life, but duty had called. And the man definitely believed in duty and justice. It was the latter he was seeking now.

As he shrugged off his uniform and stood in front of his assigned employee locker, his phone rang. It was still in the front pocket of his green work uniform. The man opened the pocket, took out his phone, and checked the number on the screen.

A frown creased his forehead, and he glanced around the room. No one had entered since he came in, but he still had to be careful. Then he pressed the answer button.

"Why are you calling me on my cell?" he rasped.

"I need to talk to you!" the voice on the other line said.

"I'll call you back in ten minutes."

He cut off the call without waiting for a response and stared silently at his locker for a moment. Then the man finished changing into his everyday clothes, hung his uniform in the locker, and secured it.

He trudged out of the building. The revolving door spun continuously—it was closing time, and most employees were headed home. No one paid him any notice. The man had found it easy to blend in with his nondescript appearance.

Once he was out on the streets, he strode quickly to the bus stop. The campus shuttle that ran through downtown Lexinbridge had just arrived, and there was a small queue waiting to file in. The man joined the queue and moved forward with it until he was at the head of the line. He stepped into the bus, tapped his bus card against the onboard fare box situated next to the driver, and walked down the aisle until he found an empty seat at the back and sat down. Three minutes later, the bus left the stop and continued its circuitous trip toward downtown.

After a little while, the man spied the corner of twenty-fourth and St. Paul street. Just where he needed to stop. He'd made several trips on this route over the years and had noticed a public pay phone with graffiti all over it tucked into a corner across the street. A quick check had confirmed that the payphone still worked, and there was no CCTV in that area.

The man pushed the touch strip on the side of the bus, and the bus pulled into the next stop. He stepped off and crossed the street to the other side. It was hard to navigate the sidewalk—teeming groups of tourists holding maps and chattering with each other mingled with office workers intent on hurrying home for dinner. The man sidestepped a stroller that almost rammed into him and moved closer to the storefronts displaying discount offers emblazoned in large neon letters.

He soon reached the payphone. There was no one using it, so the man stepped up to it, lifted the receiver from the hook, and punched in a number from memory.

"Danny, it's me," he said. "I thought we'd agreed you wouldn't call me on my cell."

"I'm sorry. I needed to talk to you immediately."

"So what's so urgent?"

"The police were here to see me. They asked if I'd seen a pin like the veteran ones we bought a while ago, and I said I had one." The man heard the sound of water being poured into a glass and swallowed. "They asked me where the pin was."

"So what did you say?"

"I told them I'd misplaced it. They asked where I'd been on Thursday, Friday, and Monday night, and I said I'd been here on duty, and they could confirm with the security office. Then they left. So what the hell did you do with my pin?"

The man rubbed his jaw. "I lost it. Don't worry, it's not a problem."

"I know I promised to help you, but I don't want this coming back on me," Danny hissed. "I called our friend at the station to find out what was going on. He checked with one of the detectives and found out a certain Marcus Tate, an investigator for one of the law firms, met with the detectives and gave them the pin that was traced back to me. Our friend figured we were in some way related to what happened, and he's asked me not to call him again." Danny sighed. "You need to take care of this. And make sure to leave me out of it. Hold on."

There was a muffled sound in the background. Then Danny came back on. "I have to go. Duty calls." The call ended.

The man put the phone receiver back on the hook, leaned against the pay phone frame, and stared off into the distance.

He knew who Marcus Tate was. He'd followed Zora Smyth for a while and had seen her talking to a man she called Marcus. It'd been easy to follow Marcus without being detected, and the man had seen him enter one of the tall luxurious buildings in downtown Lexinbridge. He'd followed him into the lobby where Marcus had pressed the button for the fifth floor. The information on the lobby wall had confirmed what he'd already guessed—Marcus had headed into Smyth Law Associates, a firm that Zora's mother owned. The man knew that because he'd done a background check on Zora once she'd gotten entangled with the case.

A cough erupted from his mouth, and he quickly pulled out a handkerchief to cover it and held it in place until the spasms stopped. He didn't need to check to know there was blood on the handkerchief. A look in the mirror in the morning had also confirmed what he'd suspected: his clothes hung more loosely on him. The disease was moving faster than he'd expected. But he couldn't stop now.

The man opened his wallet and pulled out the picture of the girl. The edges were worn, and the picture was creased in the middle, but the girl's smile shone as bright as ever. He missed her terribly. It was like an ache that held him tightly and refused to let go.

The muscle in his jaw twitched. He needed complete revenge—for her. And he couldn't afford to have anyone poking into his business until he was done. He still had one more person on his list to take care of—the worst of them all—before it was truly over. This monster might even be onto him already. The man would have to move from his apartment to the hideout he'd prepared a few months ago, to evade the monster and make it difficult for anyone to track him down.

He kissed the picture reverently and put it back into his wallet. He would have to stop Zora and Marcus. No matter how wrong it was.

The man pushed aside any prick to his conscience. He'd known it might come to this:

harming anyone that interfered. But his need to avenge the girl was greater. He had no other option.

Zora was the easier target, but an attack on her might take her off the suspect list, and that was a risk he wasn't willing to take. He needed the police to stay focused on her.

The man would have to concentrate on Marcus instead.

It was time to pay him a visit.

23

D rake paced his expansive living room. His rolled-up white dress shirt reflected the shards of the setting sunlight that flooded the space and gave an orange-like tinge to the furniture. This was one of the views he loved to watch from his penthouse, but he barely looked at it today. His mind was on the news he'd just received.

The lawyer, Calvin Faulkner, was dead. Third victim. Formalin and Rohypnol found in his bloodstream. And Drake had been one of the last people to see him alive.

He was now certain he knew what was going on. It had to be that old geezer—the girl's father. He remembered the murderous look in his eyes when they'd crossed paths at the police station last year. All three victims who had died were linked to the case. And if Drake remembered correctly, he was the only one left that was still alive, which meant the old fogey would be gunning for him next.

Drake walked to the dart cabinet on the left wall and opened it. He picked four darts, moved a few feet backward, and threw them in quick succession. All four hit the bull's eye. It was a habit he'd picked up in college. Throwing the darts helped him think while he waited for Tiny to get back to him.

It wasn't Drake's fault the girl had died. It had been a pity really. Such a waste of beauty. She should have been pleased he'd shown an interest in her. Instead, she'd chosen to take her own life. Drake didn't see how that concerned him. The others had merely tried to minimize the damage. He didn't really care about any of them, but death by injection of Formalin and Rohypnol was a terrible way to die.

His phone rang. He sauntered back to the coffee table and picked it up. "Yes?"

"We didn't find the old man in his apartment," Tiny said. "It seems he's fled already. He might have made us."

"Find him!"

"Yes, sir."

"What about the security guard?"

"We have him at the warehouse. Would you like us to wait for you?"

"I'll be there shortly." Drake ended the call.

He dropped his phone into the pocket of his black pants and headed to the door. He would take his motorcycle, the Ducati Desmosedici. Drake didn't get to take it out as often as he liked, but it was time to change that. It would get him to the warehouse quickly despite the traffic, and Tiny would bring it back home later.

Drake's face hardened. The security guard had no idea what was coming his way—he shouldn't have allied with the old geezer.

Now Drake would make an example of him.

———

Drake wiped his hands with the towel and handed it back to Tiny, who tossed it into the open fire in the drum. The other implements used had been destroyed as well. Drake never took chances. You never knew who might betray you.

It'd been a messy affair with the security guard. The man had tried to hold back as much as possible. Drake had to admire that. But he'd been no match for Drake and had given up everything he knew at the end. He'd confirmed the identity of the killer, though he didn't know the old geezer was in the wind. So much for true friends.

Drake opened the driver's door and slipped into his car. It was time to leave. Tiny would take care of the rest. The security man would end up in the river with a stone tied around his body. It would be a couple of months before they found him, and the trail would be cold by then.

He felt something dig into his back, and Drake turned and fished it out. It was Tiny's wallet—the man had a propensity to lose it. Well, Drake wouldn't give it to him this time. Tiny had to learn to be more careful with it. He could pick it up when he got back to the house.

Drake opened the glove compartment to toss it in, and a photo fell out of the wallet onto the passenger seat. It was a picture of Zora Smyth. And it wasn't the same one he had. She was relaxed, and her eyes twinkled in merriment. It looked as if the photo had been taken secretly.

A sardonic smile lit up his face. *Well, well, well. Who would have thought?* So Tiny had a crush on Miss Smyth. Now Drake needed to meet her face to face. It would be fun watching Tiny react to her presence since he'd never shown interest in any woman before.

But he had to take care of the old geezer first. Drake would have to flush him out. As long as he was still in Lexinbridge, he would be found no matter how deep he'd hidden himself. Drake was sure of that.

The corners of his lips turned up as excitement bubbled in his veins. The hunter had now become the hunted.

But that didn't mean Drake couldn't have a little fun in the meantime.

It was time to meet Miss Smyth.

24

Zora heard the distant sound of the phone ringing. She opened her eyes, blinked as her eyes adjusted, and then checked the time on the alarm clock on the bedside table. It was ten p.m. She'd fallen asleep early.

The phone rang again, and Zora reached for it and glanced at the screen. The number appeared familiar, so she tapped the answer button. "This is Zora," she said. "Who's this?"

"Hello. This is Nurse Greyson calling from Lexinbridge Regional Hospital. Do you know a Mr. Marcus Tate? You were the last call on his phone and number one on his speed dial."

Zora sat up as sleep fled from her eyes. "Yes, I do. Is everything okay?"

"He was just admitted into the ER. We were able to identify him from the ID found in his wallet, but we needed information to contact his family, so we figured we call you."

Zora jumped up from the bed. "I'll be right there in ten minutes. Thanks for calling."

"No problem."

Zora dropped her phone on the bedside table and quickly dressed in a pink and white T-shirt, jeans, and a light jacket. She grabbed her phone, wallet, and keys, and raced out of the apartment. Zora shot up a quick prayer for Marcus' safety. She needed all the help she could get.

She hailed a cab and directed the driver to head to Lexinbridge Regional Hospital. The roads were empty at that hour, so it didn't take Zora long to arrive. She paid the driver, jumped out of the cab, and sprinted toward the ER entrance. Zora darted through the automatic sliding doors and headed to the check-in station.

Lexington Regional Hospital was a Level 1 Trauma Center. It was the only one in Lexinbridge, so its ER buzzed with activity at all hours. Zora ignored the cacophony of patients, family members, and hospital staff and approached one of the nurses-on-duty at the check-in station.

"I'm looking for Mr. Marcus Tate," Zora said to the nurse. "I got a call from the hospital saying he was admitted here."

The nurse tapped the keyboard in front of her and scanned the computer screen. "What's your relationship with Mr. Tate?" she asked.

Zora thought quickly. "I'm his fiancée," she said.

"Can I see your ID please?"

Zora pulled her wallet from her jeans pocket and open it. She extracted her ID and handed it over to the nurse.

The nurse checked it out, typed some more on the keyboard, printed out a badge, and handed both the badge and ID to Zora.

"Please wear the badge at all times," she said. "He's in E13. Just go to your left and walk through that entrance." The nurse pointed to a set of double doors. "Tap your badge on the black badge reader there, and the door will open."

Zora thanked her with a smile, turned, and headed toward the east wing until she got to the entrance. She touched the badge against the card reader, and the doors swung inward.

There was a central nursing station in the middle of the area with rooms surrounding it on all sides. Most of the rooms seemed occupied, and the air bubbled with the occasional moans from patients and chatter from the nurses and doctors. Zora followed the numbering of the rooms until she got to E13.

She pulled the screen aside to see Marcus in a hospital gown lying on the bed with a bandage wrapped around his head. The dressing seemed fresh, but it was already spotted with streaks of blood. His left arm was in a sling, and and green, purple, and red bruises crisscrossed his right arm, with an IV line extending from the forearm. His eyes were closed, but his chest rose and fell rhythmically.

"He's asleep, you know." Zora turned to see a petite nurse with blond straight hair pulled up in a ponytail push a mobile cart into the room.

The tension in her shoulders eased. "How's he doing?" she asked.

"What's your relationship with the patient?"

"He is my fiancé," Zora answered, her eyes on Marcus as she moved closer.

His eyes fluttered open. "Hi, babe," Marcus said lazily.

Zora almost fell back in shock, and her face grew warm. She'd thought Marcus was asleep. She could see the amusement in his eyes, though shadows of pain lurked at the corners.

The nurse gave them both a knowing smile.

"Give me a few minutes, and I'll be out of your hair." She checked his temperature, blood pressure, and respiratory rate and noted them on a laptop on the mobile cart. She smiled at them and left, pushing the cart out of the room.

"Are you okay?" Zora asked, her eyes searching his. "When did you wake up?"

Marcus pulled himself to a sitting position on the bed. "One question at a time, little sis, or should I say *babe*?" He winked at her.

Zora felt her face heat up. She punched him on the shoulder.

"Ouch, that hurts!" he said, doubling over.

Zora reached out to touch him. "I'm sorry, so sorry. Are you okay?"

Marcus' chest shook, and the next thing she knew, he was laughing out loud.

Zora made as if to hit him again but ended up rubbing his shoulder. "You're lucky you're a patient right now, otherwise ..."

"Otherwise?" He looked at her with a smirk on his face.

She leaned closer to him, their faces only inches apart. "We'll never know, will we?" she said softly.

Zora heard his breath hitch and saw the pulse in his neck quicken. She held his gaze for a moment and then flashed him a Mona Lisa smile before moving away. She cleared away the sheets on the lower part of the bed and sat down.

"So what happened?" she asked, her voice now business-like.

Marcus leaned back on the pillows behind him. "I was coming back from a meeting with one of the HR analysts at the Collmark group," he said.

Zora's eyes snapped to his. "HR Analyst? A lady?" Marcus nodded. "How did you find her?"

He smiled, though a moment of pain crossed his face. "I have my ways."

Zora could very well guess what had happened. Marcus must have gone on a date with her. Women seemed to always fall for him. Not that she blamed them. He was tall and handsome, with the most gorgeous expressive eyes. It was like he had this magnetic beam that advertised he was single and available for grabs.

"She told me there'd been only one major HR case at the company a year ago," Marcus said. "Everything was hush hush at the time, so she didn't have all the details. But there was a rumor circulating in the company at that time that one of the new employees had been sexually assaulted by the owner's son, a vice president at the company. The employee reported the case to HR but got accused of defamation instead and was fired."

"Did she tell you the girl's name?"

"Anna Hammond. She remembered the name because she'd heard the girl committed suicide not long after. I was shocked the company would cover up something as serious as that."

Zora was silent as she twirled a strand of her hair. In her opinion, rape was one of the worst assaults a a person could inflict on another—it violated every aspect of the victim's life. If it was true the girl had been assaulted, that was more than enough reason for someone in the girl's life to seek revenge.

"You look cute doing that."

"Huh?" Zora looked up to see Marcus grinning at her. She smacked his thigh.

"Ouch!" he said as he used his right hand to rub the spot. Then his eyes grew serious. "If someone did that to someone dear to me, I'd make them pay," he said in a low voice.

Zora understood the sentiment. Marcus was fiercely loyal and would seek justice if someone close to him was wronged.

After a moment, he continued, "Once we went our separate ways, I decided to take the subway for a change instead of calling for a cab. As I passed a dark alley on my way there, someone hit me on the head with what seemed like a tire iron. I was dizzy but managed to managed to grab his hand when he swung at me again. The attacker appeared to be in his late fifties from his stature—his face was covered with a mask, and he was wearing a hooded jacket—but he had the strength of a young man.

"But the attacker didn't stop. He used his left hand to deliver punch after punch to my stomach and sides. I almost passed out from the pain, but I held on to that right arm with everything in me. I knew if I let go, I'd be done. Someone passing by heard the scuffle and called out, which made the attacker run away. The same person called nine-one-one before I passed out. I woke five minutes ago to find myself in the hospital."

"Do you think it was the killer?" Zora asked.

"Honestly, I don't know," he said. "Maybe—"

"He found out you provided information to the police," Zora completed.

Marcus nodded. "That's the only reason that makes sense," he said.

Zora shivered. The only way the killer could have found Marcus was if he was watching or following him. What if he was watching Zora as well? She shivered again.

"Don't worry, I'll be fine," he said in a soft tone. "I'll be more careful next time. We both need to be. And it's not so bad—just a sprain and a few bruises. I'm made of hardy stock, you know." He swung his right hand behind his head and leaned back. "Now I can slack off," he said with a lazy smile.

Zora burst out laughing. She knew he was trying to make her feel better.

He grinned and tried to sit back up, but a flash of pain crossed his face, and he collapsed back on the bed.

Zora pretended not to notice. Instead, she stifled a yawn.

"Now, *babe*, Marcus said. "I think you should go home and sleep, since we both need the rest."

"Hey! I had to get in here somehow." She picked a pillow from the foot of the bed and threw it at his head.

Marcus ducked, and the pillow flew over him. He laughed at her embarrassment.

Her face warmed. "Sorry I lied," she said sheepishly.

"It's fine," he said.

Time seemed to freeze as they stared at each other, until Zora cleared her throat. Marcus flushed and rubbed the back of his neck.

Zora hid a smile and rose to her feet. *Who would have thought Marcus could be this cute?* "I'll come and see you tomorrow," she said as she moved backward toward the door.

Marcus nodded and smiled at her.

She gave him a final wave and then exited the room.

As she walked out of the hospital, Zora thought about what Marcus had shared. She could feel the pieces clicking into place. And just in time too before her name got leaked out to the public.

All they needed to do now was find out more about Anna Hammond.

And hopefully, they'd find the killer.

25

The old man in the hooded jacket sat alone at the table at the back of the diner and faced the entrance. The thick smell of onions and barbecue smoke hung low in the air. The waitress, a boxy woman with long dark tresses, had delivered his usual order—mashed potatoes with gravy, and coleslaw, and a glass of orange juice, but he'd been a regular enough customer that she knew to leave him alone after that.

He'd called his old friend, Danny, but there'd been no response. If he had to take a guess, he would assume that the monster had gotten to him. It wasn't what he'd planned for, since his friend had been on his side. But there was nothing he could do about it now.

The man had been fortunate to leave his apartment when he did. He was sure the place was turned upside down by now. But they wouldn't find anything. He'd gotten rid of all personal items months ago, except the ones he kept on his person all the time. And the man had practiced his martial arts long enough to be able to do the exercises on his own.

He took a sip of the orange juice and grimaced. It had a sour note to it. He pushed around the food with his fork since it didn't hold his interest as usual.

The man's mind slipped back to earlier that evening. The investigator was tough. He'd expected him to pass out once he'd hit him with the tire iron, but Marcus had fought back. It didn't matter though —he hadn't planned to kill him. The attack was only meant to be a warning. The man had followed the ambulance to the hospital where he'd confirmed the investigator would be out of commission for a few days. That was what he'd wanted. For them to stop digging, long enough for the man to finish what he'd started.

He wasn't worried about what that monster, Drake Pierce, was up to. Drake would be caught in the man's web no matter how much he schemed or how much protection he had around him. He had a weakness, and the man was going to exploit it and destroy him through it.

The cops were not an obstacle to what he planned to do. They were too overworked and slow, and he'd be long gone by the time they solved the case.

That left Zora as the only other person who could interfere. He hoped she'd gotten his message loud and clear from the attack on Marcus, but he might have to make sure.

Now that he'd made a decision, the man picked up his fork and dug into his food.

The tasty flavors exploded in his mouth with his appetite restored.

26

Zora yawned as the cab stopped in front of her apartment. She paid the driver and got out. She was exhausted since she'd had a rough night after returning from the hospital and had dragged her tired self to class. Zora had ended up with two classes and two labs in the morning and had spent the afternoon at one of the school's community clinics. She hadn't been able to concentrate in any one of them.

All she could think about was Marcus and the attack. As much as Zora wanted to solve the case, she didn't like anyone close to her getting hurt in the process. Marcus had tried to hide how terrible he'd felt, but Zora could see he was in a lot of pain.

"Good afternoon, Miss Smyth."

Zora turned to see a tall, muscular bald man with a massive build standing a few feet from her next to a black Rolls Royce Phantom. He looked intimidating, clad in black on black button-down shirt and pants. The jagged scar on his face didn't help matters.

"Who are you, and how do you know my name?" Zora asked.

"My boss, Drake Pierce, would like to see you."

Zora racked her brain. The name sounded familiar. Suddenly, it came to her. Collmark group. The son that Silas had advised her to avoid at all costs.

She took a step backward. "Why does he want to see me?"

"Since you recognize the name, you can probably guess why." The man moved toward her.

"If you take another step, I'm going to scream!" By now, two of her neighbors were on the sidewalk and giving them curious glances. One of them pulled out his cell phone.

"My boss means no harm," the man said. "He just wants to have a chat with you."

Before Zora knew it, the man was now beside her and was strong-arming her toward the car.

Panic swelled up in her, and her pulse jumped. Without thinking, Zora opened her mouth and bit a chunk of the man's arm.

The man yelped in surprise and let her go.

Zora took off in the direction of her apartment and didn't look back. She sprinted up the stairs, unlocked her door with shaky hands, and slammed the door behind her, setting the bolt in place.

She leaned against the door and took deep breaths to calm herself. Her hand gripped the pendant around her neck. How had she gotten on Drake Pierce's radar? What did he want with her? And why was this man trying to force her to see him?

Her hands couldn't stop shaking. She needed to call Marcus. She looked down and noticed her book bag was still on her shoulder. Zora was surprised she hadn't dropped it outside. She turned it upside down until her phone fell out along with her other items. She picked it up and dialed Marcus' number.

"Hi, Marcus," Zora said, her voice trembling.

"Zora, are you okay?"

"I'll be fine. I just had a visit from Drake Pierce."

"Wait. What?"

"The man tried to grab me," Zora's voice choked. She slid down the door to the floor.

She heard rustling in the background. "Where are you? I'm coming now."

Zora sniffled. "I'm in my apartment. No, you don't need to come. I think he's gone."

"I'm coming right now."

"Please don't," Zora said in a whisper. "I need some time alone."

"Zora!"

"Please."

"Did you call the cops?"

"I don't want the cops. It could become more complicated."

"Okay. But I'll send a security detail to you. It's someone you already know and recognize. I'll ask him to wait outside your apartment until whenever you're ready to see him."

"Thanks."

"Zora, don't you think you should tell your mom what's going on by now?"

"No! You can't tell her!"

"Okay, okay, I won't. That's your decision to make. You're sure you don't need me there?"

"I'll be fine. Maybe come by later this evening."

"I'll be there."

Thanks, Marcus. You know, for everything."

"No worries, little sis, or should I say *babe*?"

Zora chuckled. "Marcus!"

"It's nice to hear you laugh. I'll send the guy over now. Try and rest a bit, okay? See you later."

"Thanks." Zora ended the call.

She stayed huddled at the door, closed her eyes, and rested her head on her knees.

Zora opened her eyes to see she was still crouched at the door. She'd lost track of time and had nodded off to sleep. Zora placed a hand against the door and dragged herself up. Her legs tingled, and as she tried to work out the cramp in her left calf, her feet brushed against what felt like paper.

She looked down and saw a white envelope. Zora didn't remember it being there when she'd left this morning—it must have been pushed under the door and into the apartment. She bent down and picked up the envelope. The envelope was sealed but addressed to her in a scribbled handwriting she didn't recognize. She took it to the kitchen countertop and tore it open.

A single sheet of folded paper landed on the granite surface.

Zora picked it up and opened it. Words written in red ink jumped out at her:

This is your second warning. You and your loved ones might not be so lucky next time.

Her pulse ratcheted up a notch, and she gripped the edge of the island to steady herself.

The attack on Marcus had been a warning to her. She was responsible for what had happened to Marcus.

Zora wanted to scream so badly, but the neighbors wouldn't approve. Instead, she took a series of deep breaths until she felt herself grow calmer. Then she moved over to the couch and sat down.

She was sick and tired of everything. People around her were getting hurt, and she still needed her life back.

Something had to give.

She thought for a moment. On one hand, if Zora stopped digging into the case, she could end up a victim for a crime she didn't commit, and her life would be over. On the other hand, if she continued, someone close to her could be seriously injured or killed. But the truth could come out as well, and the real killer could be found and stopped.

Zora rubbed her hands over her face. *Aargh*. There was no clear-cut option to choose. And she was too tired to be making such decisions. She got up, walked over to one of her kitchen cabinets, and pulled out a quart-sized Ziploc bag. Zora placed the note and the envelope in it and dropped it into her book bag.

She'd show Marcus the note when she saw him later today, and they could discuss and settle on a workable plan, since two heads were better than one. In the meantime, it wouldn't hurt to find out more about the Anna Hammond case.

Zora trudged to her room and switched on the computer on her desk. She sat down in her chair and began to hunt for any news on Anna Hammond, going down the list of search results until she found a news report that seemed to fit. She opened it in a new tab and began to read.

Anna Hammond had been found hanging over the edge of the rooftop of the Collmark building, a thick rope around her neck and the other end secured to the roof hatch's railing system. The case had been ruled a suicide. Zora looked at the picture included in the article. She saw a gorgeous, innocent-looking young lady with sparkling blue eyes and a soft smile. It had been a tragic death.

Zora closed the tab and scrolled down the previous search results, but there were no other related articles.

That's strange. News about a death on such a prominent building in the city would have been widespread and discussed for days by the news media. She kept searching and even tried other keywords but found nothing.

Zora leaned back and folded her arms. She needed to find out more about the case. *Think, Zora, think.* She tapped her right fingers against her arm and stared at the ceiling.

Then it occurred to her.

The best way would be to hear about it straight from the horse's mouth.

Zora reached for her phone.

There was no time to waste, and maybe Marcus could make it happen today.

27

"What did you say?"

"I'm sorry I couldn't get her to come," Tiny said. "The neighbors were everywhere, and I didn't want to draw any unnecessary attention to us."

Drake stifled a chuckle. "And she bit your arm."

"Yes." Tiny scowled.

Drake let out a loud laugh. This was getting more interesting. Tiny had failed. And he never failed.

"Do you want me to go back and try again?" Tiny asked.

Drake dismissed him with a wave. "Hold off for now." He inclined his head toward the door.

Tiny left the room and shut the door behind him.

Drake relaxed back on the black swivel chair. He

was working from his home office today. Since he'd planned to meet Zora, he'd figured his penthouse was better than meeting her at the company office. For one, it had more privacy.

His mouth turned up in a smile. Drake had never expected Zora to be a she-cat. Feisty. Just the way he liked them. And more reason to try and make her his queen. She would make a great conquest. But to be able to play with her properly, he had to take care of the other problem first.

The smile left his face. The old geezer. They hadn't found him yet.

Drake slammed his fists on his desk. He would capture that fogey no matter what it took or how deep he hid. Drake was looking forward to squeezing the life out of him.

His mind went back to Zora, and his fists relaxed. How he wished she was here. Drake would have loved to play with her. It would have been a great way to let out the tension he'd built from all the stock trades he'd made this morning. Drake had tripled his investments, but he was tired.

Maybe it was time to see Susie.

She was always game for any adventure.

28

"T hanks for coming," Marcus told the detective.

Detective Monte was a detective in the special victims unit at the local PD and had been on the force for twenty-five years. The buzz cut he sported hinted at a military service in a past life, and a handle bar mustache completed his look. It was obvious Detective Monte was meticulous about his appearance with his dark blue polo shirt tucked into tan chinos and highly polished Italian shoes.

Zora sat at a table adjacent to theirs and listened in on the conversation. She knew her shadow was nearby. He was as good as Marcus had claimed he'd be, and she was thankful for it.

The bistro was packed full, with every table

taken. It bustled with waiters carrying trays piled high with assorted homemade breads, sandwiches, chicken sliders, and beverages. Clad in a black base-ball cap over a pink and black T-shirt and blue jeans, Zora had arrived before Marcus and the detective and had been lucky to snag two tables. She pulled the baseball cap further down to cover her face.

"I wouldn't be here if I didn't owe you one," the detective said. "Things are tense at the station because of the Formalin Killer, so I won't be able to stay for long."

"Is that what they're calling him now?" Marcus rubbed the band-aid on his forehead that had replaced the bandage around his head.

"Well, three people seemed to have died so far from formalin injections." The detective took a sip of the coffee Marcus had ordered for him. "I heard you were attacked, but you seem none the worse for wear."

Marcus lifted his sling toward the detective. "If this is your definition of 'none the worse for wear,' then, yes, I'm doing good," he said.

"So what do you want to know?" Monte leaned back on the seat and fingered his mustache.

"Could you tell me about the Anna Hammond case? I heard you were the lead detective on it."

Monte tugged at his mustache. "Hmmm. No one has asked me about this case in a long time. Why do you want to know? Did you find any new information?" He leaned forward, his eyes sparkling with interest.

"Just curious," Marcus said.

The detective's eyes searched Marcus' face for a moment, and then a faraway look came into them as he leaned back. "I'll never forget the case. Her face in death still gives me nightmares. Sweet young thing. In her early twenties. She'd just started working at the Collmark group not too long before then. Her father was pretty broken up about it."

Zora's ears perked up. "Her father?" Marcus asked.

"Yes, he was the only family she had. There were no siblings or other relatives."

"Do you know anything more about the father?"

"All I know is that he works as a janitor at the medical school."

Zora felt a shiver run down her spine at those words. She didn't think it was a coincidence.

"What's his name?"

The detective rubbed his jaw. "I believe it was Alfred Pickles."

A sudden coldness ripped through Zora. *It was the janitor!*

"But her name was Anna Hammond," Marcus said.

"Yes, I believe he changed her name when she was a kid. He didn't want the others making fun of her. Hammond was his mother's maiden name. He raised her alone after her mother abandoned her, and neighbors said they were close. The man was pretty broken up about her death. It was like the light went out of his eyes, and he became a shadow of himself."

"Do you know what made her commit suicide?" Marcus asked.

"It seemed she'd caught the eye of the owner's son at the Collmark group. Drake Pierce. Nasty piece of work. An animal really. Has beady eyes too, as far as I'm concerned. I hear the ladies like him, but I don't know what they see in him.

"She had reported at the ER that Drake raped her at a company dinner. But the rape kit disappeared, and the CCTV footage at the restaurant where the rape was said to have occurred had been erased. The bar claimed they had some sort of malfunction, so there was no way to prove he was the perp. When she filed a formal complaint at the company, she got fired instead. She couldn't find work anywhere else too—it seemed she'd been blacklisted at other companies. She committed suicide two weeks after it happened."

"Was it confirmed a suicide?"

"Well, there wasn't any evidence of foul play. Not sure how she gained entrance to the building since they'd taken away her ID. I guess she hung herself there as a last outcry against the injustice." The detective sipped his cup of coffee. "Most people we talked to only had good things to say about her. It was a real tragedy.

"What struck me though was that there was pressure from above to close the case. It didn't sit right with me, but what could I do?" He drained his cup of coffee. "Darn it, you shouldn't have made me talk about this case. Brings back bad memories."

"Sorry about that."

The detective waved Marcus' concern away and looked at his watch. "I need to head back now. Thanks for the coffee." He stood up.

"See you around," Marcus said.

The detective re-tucked his shirt into his pants and stepped out of the bistro.

After the detective left, Zora sidled up to Marcus's table and claimed the vacated seat. "Such a terrible story," she said. "Are you thinking what I'm thinking?"

"Yes," Marcus said. "Alfred Pickles. He's most likely the killer. He has a strong motive for wanting the people who hurt his daughter dead."

"And he works at the Gross Anatomy lab. He had motive and opportunity."

"Yes, that too."

"I think I now have a good idea of how the professor fits in," Zora said. "Maybe he had something to do with the missing rape kit. It requires a person with significant authorization for the record to have disappeared from the system."

"Maybe if the police searched his office and his house, they might find something related to the rape kit."

"I agree."

Marcus probed her with a penetrating gaze. "So how do you feel?"

"I'm angry that Alfred Pickles nudged the detectives toward me." Zora sighed. "But most of all, I'm just relieved it's almost over. I can get my life back. So what do we do next?"

"I'm not sure it's over yet."

Zora frowned. "What do you mean?"

"I heard from a source at the courts that Morris has applied for a warrant for your arrest."

Zora jumped up. "Are you kidding me?" she said,

her voice a little louder than appropriate. She noticed several eyes swivel toward her from the other tables, and her face grew warm at the attention.

Marcus extended a hand toward her. "Zora, sit. I haven't finished."

Zora sat down slowly. By now, the other customers had returned to their meals.

Marcus ran his right hand through his hair. "Silas knows the judge and has told him what's been going on so far, so the judge has agreed to delay the issuance until tomorrow, as long as we bring in evidence to support out theory. So we have to break this case wide open today."

Zora held her head in her hands. How would that happen? "Unbelievable!"

"Zora, look at me."

She lifted her head and met his eyes. She could see strength and determination shining through them to her.

Marcus held her hands. "We have all the pieces. We will end it today. It will be over. And you will be fine, you hear me?"

Zora nodded. "I won't let Pickles or Morris do this to me!"

"I'll tell the police about this." Marcus gave her a stern look. "Do not approach Pickles no matter what.

He's dangerous. We don't have any evidence now, and we don't want any potential evidence to disappear. Let the cops handle it. Promise me, okay?"

"I promise. How's your arm?"

Marcus looked down at his left arm in its sling. "It's fine. I'll be right as rain in a few days."

"I'm sorry."

"Don't be. It's not your fault. Just promise me you won't go after Pickles."

"I already said I won't."

"Good." Marcus got up. "I need to head down to the station. Let me drop you off at home."

Zora rose to her feet and followed him out of the bistro.

But she worried if they could resolve the case on time, or if they'd end up a step too late.

29

A pair of cold eyes followed Zora and Marcus as they left the bistro.

Alfred Pickles' nostrils flared. He could see his warning had gone unheeded. They'd found out about him and now wanted the cops to arrest him today. But that wasn't going to happen.

Pickles hadn't expected Zora to make the connection so soon. He'd hung around her building after dropping off the note to see how she'd react and had been surprised when she'd left with a new bodyguard. He hadn't expected that. Pickles had then followed them to this bistro and grabbed the closest table he could get without exposing himself.

Of course, they hadn't recognized him. He was wearing a blond wig, a pair of glasses, and an Italian suit. Pickles looked more like a businessman than a janitor, and had pretended he was reading a newspaper the whole time Marcus and the detective had conversed.

He remembered the cop. Detective Monte. He was good people. He'd tried to solve Anna's case, but he'd had to close it due to lack of evidence.

Pickles' skin itched where the wig touched his forehead, and he rubbed the area. He'd only followed them here on a whim, but hearing their conversation had changed everything.

He hadn't wanted to go after either of them, but Pickles' plans had changed as soon as he'd discovered how far they'd cracked the case. He couldn't let them expose him, not right now.

Hurting Marcus would not solve the problem, though he'd convinced a friend of his in the underworld—as he'd listened to their discussion—who owed him a favor, to ensure Marcus had a minor accident after he dropped Zora off. He hoped it would prevent Marcus from getting to the station soon and give Pickles enough time to execute the remainder of his plans.

But Zora was the real threat here and would not give up even if Marcus was harmed. He wasn't sure if she was stupid or fearless. It didn't help she reminded him of someone he detested, the person who'd broken all that he'd held dear and abandoned him. And she'd unearthed his role in the murders. Now Zora had to pay the price for her choices.

A cough seized his throat, and he found it difficult to breathe. Pickles tried to suppress it since he didn't need the extra attention a coughing episode like this might bring. The last thing he wanted was for people to remember him, especially when he'd already been careful to stay away from the cameras. He suspected the cops might come here after his plan for Zora was executed, since it was one of the last places she'd have been in, and he didn't want to stand out. People tended to recall the oddest things.

He took as big a deep breath as he could draw into his lungs and turned his thoughts back to the matters at hand. He would take care of Zora first, and then finish off Drake Pierce, that monster whose eyes and genitals Pickles had already gouged out in the picture he carried in his pocket. Drake thought he was safe with his security detail, but Pickles had already figured out a way to get to him.

But Zora's bodyguard posed a problem. The guy looked dangerous, and Pickles wasn't convinced he could overpower him—he'd grown weaker in the last twenty-four hours. So he needed a way to separate them from each other.

A plan came to mind, and the more he ruminated on it, the more Pickles was sure it would work. The anticipated gap in the schedule would be more than enough for what he had in mind.

He rose to his feet.

It was time to get Zora Smyth out of the way for good.

30

M arcus dropped Zora off in front of her apartment. As she climbed up the stairs, she heard another car slide into the parking space he'd just vacated—Zora was certain it was her bodyguard.

She opened the door to her apartment and dropped her bag on the couch before heading to the kitchen and opening the refrigerator to grab a bottle of water.

Her throat was parched. Zora downed the water and placed the empty bottle on the granite countertop.

Then her doorbell rang.

Zora strode to the door and peeked through the peephole. "Who is it?" she asked.

"It's me, Ted." Ted was her new bodyguard.

"What is it?"

"I need to leave briefly. I'll be back in about seven minutes. Please do not open the door for anyone in that time."

"I won't. Thanks for letting me know."

"No problem."

Zora heard his footsteps recede as he moved away from the door and headed down the stairs.

She padded back to her couch and dropped into it. Zora was exhausted, but she could see the light at the end of the tunnel. Morris would fail to get his arrest warrant, and she'd get her life back.

Zora wished she could talk to someone right now about it, but Marcus was busy with ending the case, Silas had a lot on his plate, and her mother wasn't even an option. She wasn't sure if Christina was home. She'd had an extremely hectic schedule this week, and they'd been shorthanded at work. Still, Christina had tried to call Zora as much as she could, though she always sounded tired. She'd be off for a few days from tomorrow, and they'd promised to have lunch together.

She ambled toward Christina's room and opened the door. The bed was made, and nothing was out of place. It seemed Christina hadn't returned from work.

Her doorbell rang, and Zora turned and glanced at

the door. She wasn't expecting anyone since she typically didn't receive many visitors at her apartment.
But she wondered if Ted was back already.

Zora strode to the door and looked through the
peephole. There was a blond man wearing a UPS
uniform and cap and holding a large box in his hands.

Though Ted had warned her not to open for
anyone, Zora had bought some winter outfits online
from her favorite designer a few days ago, and the
package could distract her for now.

She slid back the bolt and opened the door. "Yes,
can I help you?"

"I have a package for Zora Smyth," the man said.
The voice sounded familiar. Zora tried to think of
where she'd heard it before. "Miss?"

"Sorry, you were saying?"

"Please sign here," the man said, pointing to the
clipboard.

As Zora moved to take the proffered pen, she felt
a needle push into her arm.

Her eyes widened, and she gasped and staggered.
She tried to scramble back into her apartment and
slam the door, but the man held her arm in a steely
grip. Zora turned and headbutted him and heard the
crunch of bone shattering as she broke his nose.

The man howled, and his grip on her arm loosened.

Zora managed to get back inside her apartment and started to push her door shut, but the man had forced his shoulder into the doorway. She could feel herself weakening as she struggled to close it.

"You should have heeded my warning," the man said in a harsh tone.

Her eyes widened, and Zora lost focus for a second.

It was all the time the man needed. He gave a sudden hard push against the door, slamming Zora behind it. She felt herself go down.

The man reached to seize her. Zora kicked at him, but he swatted her leg away like it was an annoying fly.

He grabbed and turned her, and held both arms in a lock. Zora struggled to break his hold, but she couldn't. She felt her strength seeping away. She tried to scream, but her voice had lost its power.

As he tightened his hold on her, Zora suddenly felt like she was swimming under water. She shook her head to drive away the effect, but it was no use.

Zora's body grew limp, and then her vision dimmed and went out.

31

D rake rapped his fingers on the armrest as he sat in the back seat of his Rolls Royce. Tiny was driving him home. He knew he needed to be more careful these days since all attempts to find Alfred Pickles had been in vain.

Tiny and his team had been out at all hours combing through the city and looking for him. There'd been no credit card charges, and his employer had reported he'd turned in his resignation letter and left.

But Drake wasn't afraid. They would find him sooner or later, and the man would pay for the inconvenience he'd put Drake through. In the meantime, Drake had increased his security detail. Anyone who tried to get close to him would be shot first and questioned later.

The workday had been a long one for Drake. *Those incompetent fools.* He would have lost a lot of money if he hadn't caught the mistake. By the time Drake had left the office, the manager who'd been responsible for the error was long gone with security escorting him immediately from the building. Drake didn't suffer fools.

He yawned and loosened his tie. His bones felt weary, and he needed to unwind. Drake didn't have the energy to chase down Zora Smyth, but Susie would be the perfect antidote. He'd called her earlier in the day to let her know he might drop by, and he'd informed her he was on his way once he'd left the office.

Drake smiled at the thought of her. He was shocked a mature woman like her would make him feel this way—he generally preferred girls in their twenties. He'd asked her to move into one of his houses, but she'd refused, stating she preferred her own apartment. That was one of the things he liked about her—her independent spirit, not like all those empty-headed dolls who said yes to everything.

He didn't mind her place. Furnished in lush

Moroccan designs, the apartment was welcoming, and the warm colors of the drapes and rugs combined with its comfortable decor created the perfect ambience to sit back and absorb her ministrations. Drake got excited just thinking about what she'd do to him. Based on how she performed tonight, he might buy that expensive pearl necklace he'd caught her admiring in the magazine in her apartment. He'd recognized the name of the jeweler—one of the most expensive in the city.

Drake tapped on the privacy partition, and the panel receded.

"Yes, sir?" Tiny asked.

"Get a move on it."

"Will do."

The partition rose back into place as the car accelerated.

Drake leaned back and licked his lips. Nothing could stand in the way of the enjoyment he expected tonight.

32

S usie applied the make-up deftly and smiled at the face that stared back at her: delicate features with long eyelashes that laced gracefully over her eyes, a pert nose, and a generous mouth that smiled often. The years had been kind to her. She looked younger than her age, courtesy of her genes, and good exercise had helped her remain that way. The result was a body men always longed for.

She'd wanted to be an actress, but the years spent pursuing that dream had never panned out. So Susie had sought out other ways to supplement her income. Her demand had increased over the years, and it'd finally been enough to catch the attention of the H Club. Now she made so much money she didn't need any other distractions. One night alone was enough to cover her rent, and her place was not cheap.

Susie had become a little tired of the rodeo and had wanted a more permanent arrangement. She'd been lucky to catch the eye of Drake. He was young, dashing, and smart, with lots of money. All the criteria she'd been looking for. She'd heard the rumors he was the guy to be with. He was going places, and she wanted to go along for the ride. Drake had made no secret of the fact that he didn't want to share her with anyone else. Susie had obliged, and the arrangement had been working well for them both.

So it was unfortunate she had to do this. It would mean letting go of her dreams and all she'd built over the years. But she couldn't forget the little girl with the blue eyes. Those eyes had haunted her every night since last year.

Susie had to go through with it before she changed her mind.

Her doorbell rang. *It must be Drake*, she thought. He'd called to let her know he was on the way, and now her skin tingled in anticipation of seeing him. Drake always had this effect on her.

But it was time to put on her best performance. Most people didn't know, but Drake had a mean streak under that genial smile. She had to be careful not to get caught.

Susie opened the door, and there he stood, as handsome as ever. She could never grow tired of looking at him. Susie drew him into her apartment after giving him a deep kiss and shut the door behind him. His bodyguard, Tiny, would wait on the other side of the door as usual until Drake was ready to go home. He never stayed over at her place.

She led him to the large couch and helped him remove his jacket. "How was your day?" she asked him.

"Not so terrible," Drake replied.

"I'll make it better."

"That's my girl."

Susie placed his jacket on the coffee table. "Would you like something to drink?"

"Sure. A glass of water."

Susie almost stumbled as she stepped into her kitchen. Drake always requested wine, and she'd prepared with that in mind. She hadn't thought about how it would work with water, but the man had assured her that the powder was both odorless and colorless.

She opened her cabinet, pulled out a glass, and then grabbed a bottle of water from the refrigerator.

Drake only drank spring water, so Susie always kept them stacked in her refrigerator just in case.

Her hand shook as she twisted the cover off the bottle and poured the water into the glass. She looked across to where Drake sat and saw his eyes had closed. *He must be really exhausted*, she thought.

Susie quickly poured the powder into the glass and stirred it with a wooden coffee stirrer. The water looked unchanged, but she wasn't sure how it tasted. Susie slipped the stirrer and the packet under a towel on the counter—she would dispose of them later.

And looked up to see Drake staring at her.

Her heart pounded loudly against her chest, but she held her smile in place. Susie wasn't sure if he'd seen her.

She lifted the glass and carried it over to where he sat. "Here you go," she said.

"What took you so long?" he asked.

"I noticed the glass I picked at first was chipped, so I needed a new one," she lied.

"Make sure you change the whole set tomorrow."

"I will," Susie said as she handed the glass over to him.

Drake looked at her for a moment, assessing her.

She hid her discomfort and smiled, placing a hand on his thigh and squeezing it. She saw his pupils widen in anticipation of the pleasure to come. He quickly downed the water and grasped her firmly. As she whispered sweet nothings into his ear, his grip weakened and eventually slacked off.

Susie laid him gently on the couch and listened to his chest. He was still breathing. She pinched him, but he barely responded. *Good*.

She switched on the music. It was a waltz piece Susie liked to dance to with Drake. She'd been surprised to learn that Drake loved to dance, and this music was one of his favorites. It would mask the noise well.

Susie headed to a large window in the guest room at the back of the apartment and opened it. The man was waiting. He climbed into the apartment with an extra large suitcase and carried it into the living room.

He didn't say a word to her. She understood. He detested her for what she'd done to him.

Susie helped him stuff Drake into the suitcase as soundlessly as possible, all the while looking at the door. She was afraid of Tiny and couldn't imagine what would happen if he barged in.

The man was grunting heavily as they squeezed Drake's legs into the suitcase. He looked thinner than the last time she'd seen him. Maybe he was sick. But she didn't ask. It wasn't her business.

The man dragged the suitcase back to the window, pushed it onto the fire escape, and then followed after it.

Susie closed the window but didn't lock it. She went back into her kitchen and poured powder from a second packet into the remaining water in the bottle and shook it. Susie picked up the empty packet and the items she'd stuffed under the towel and hid them in a small crevice behind the refrigerator where they wouldn't be found.

Then she washed her hands, poured the water from the bottle into a second glass for herself, drank it, and then laid on the couch as she waited to drift into unconsciousness.

Susie had done her part.

The rest was up to him.

Zora opened her eyes to see herself in a dark musty room. She tried to move but couldn't. Her hands and feet were strapped with metallic cuffs to a stainless-steel table, and her body felt weak. She wriggled her feet—they were bare and toppled a glass beaker placed next to a stainless-steel surgical bowl. Thankfully, the beaker didn't break since Zora didn't need glass cuts on her feet on top of everything else.

She was fully clothed. That was a relief. Her throat tingled from the faint scents of formaldehyde in the air. Zora figured she was in a medical or a science building. She glanced up and shivered—a large cleaver knife loomed overhead, held up by a modified body scale that hung from the ceiling.

Her heart pounded as she recalled what had last happened.

She'd been injected with some substance and kidnapped by Pickles.

And there'd been no time to alert anyone. They didn't know she was missing. Ted probably hadn't realized she was gone and would have assumed she was sleeping. And it might be too late by the time Christina returned from work and raised the alarm. She wasn't sure what would happen to her now, but Zora guessed she might not make it out alive.

Tears pooled in her eyes.

After a moment, she lifted her chin. Her life could not be over just yet. Zora was a fighter. She had to find a way to escape.

She blinked back the tears, and her neck creaked as her eyes darted back and forth, searching for any escape options. She could see she was in some type of basement. There was rusty-looking surgical equipment along the walls and the corners of the room, and an outdated autopsy sink ran across the entire left wall. *Most likely a medical building then.*

There was a narrow window high up on the wall above the autopsy sink. Even if Zora managed to break free of the cuffs and by some miracle reached the window, there was no way she could squeeze through it. So that option was out. This was the one time Zora wished she was slender.

There was a large steel door on her far right, but it looked solid and dense, and Zora didn't think she could breach it without a key. So that escape route was a no go.

The sound of a metal instrument clattering on a hard surface echoed through the room.

Zora's head jerked upward in the direction of the noise. A man stood hunched over a table, his back to her. He was wearing a black hooded jacket with the hood thrown back to reveal steel grey hair chopped into a crew cut.

The man seemed to sense her eyes on him and turned to look at her.

She stiffened, and her eyes widened.

It was Alfred Pickles. The janitor. The man who'd pointed the case in her direction and made her life miserable for the last few days.

Zora's face tightened, and she ground her teeth. She wished she'd never met him at the Gross Anatomy lab.

His face was cast in stone and crossed with deep furrows as if they'd been excavated. Black eyes devoid of emotion stared back at her. A set of bandaids were splayed across his nose.

The place were she'd hit him.

"It's you!" Zora said.

The man stayed silent.

"Where am I, and why did you bring me here?" she demanded.

Pickles laid down what he'd been fiddling with and headed in her direction. When he reached her side, he said in a dry voice, "So you're awake." His dark, soulless eyes stared back at her.

Zora shivered. Panic rose in her throat, and she struggled against the restraints. "Get these off me!"

"Don't waste your energy," he said. "You won't be able to break free. And no one can hear you."

"What do you want from me?"

"From you? Nothing. I just needed you to stay out of my business. I *warned* you to stay away! But you couldn't, could you?"

Zora's breath left her at the smoldering anger in his eyes. She didn't understand why the guy hated her. She was the victim here.

She took a deep breath and forced herself to stay calm. It was more important she stayed alive than argue with him. She had to distract him for as long as possible, with something, anything.

Her eyes swung back to the area where he'd been working. A silver picture frame rested on a table adjacent to it. It was the same picture that had been in the news report. Anna Hammond.

"She's beautiful," Zora said.

The man followed her gaze. Zora could see the longing and agony on his face.

"She was the light of my life," he said. "And those monsters took her away from me."

"You mean Professor Oakley?"

"Him and all the others. Drake Pierce, Calvin Faulkner, who covered for him in exchange for a new job, and Martha Adams, who squelched the harassment report just for the sake of a promotion. My daughter meant nothing to them. And they made sure she never got another job. But it only got worse after that. She found out she could no longer have children and had been damaged from the rape. They ruined her life!"

The man grabbed the beaker at her feet and threw it against the wall. It ricocheted off the bare surface and shattered on the concrete floor, tiny crystals dispersing everywhere.

Zora shrunk into herself as the man shook with fury. She needed to be more careful.

"And my little angel changed," Pickles continued in a faraway voice. It was like he was no longer with Zora but somewhere else in his memories. "Gone was the bright cheerful girl. She became so withdrawn and fearful. All her friends and co-workers abandoned her. And there was nothing I could do to help her. Nothing I said worked. I failed her."

Zora saw the anguish reflected on his face. She knew that look. She'd felt that way when her sister disappeared.

"So she lost hope and killed herself. Do you know that rapist bastard had the guts to come to her funeral?" The muscles in Pickles' jaw twitched. "He was there laughing and drinking like nothing happened. I couldn't believe it. My daughter was lying dead in a coffin while that bastard was having a good time.

"The police couldn't do anything." Pickles' face morphed into anger. "There was no evidence. Nothing. Zilch."

He stayed silent for a moment. "A month later, a note was sent to me at work which said my daughter's rape kit had disappeared after Professor Oakley visited the forensic lab. I traced the person who sent it, and he told me what happened. He'd seen Professor Oakley removing it. He'd been afraid and resigned after it happened, so the police hadn't known about it.

"And then I heard about Martha Adams' promotion and Calvin Faulkner's new job right after Anna's death. Anna had mentioned their names after she'd first filed the employee complaint. They'd moved on with their lives like nothing happened! And that's when I swore I would make them pay for their sins. They needed to experience the same terror of helplessness before dying."

"Is that why you used Rohypnol and formalin?" Zora had to keep Pickles talking to buy more time.

He shrugged as if it meant nothing to him. "Rohypnol, to weaken and paralyze them first. Ironic, isn't it? And easy to get from Mexico. And then came the shot of formalin. I watched their masks of horror and pain as their bodies shut down."

Zora couldn't imagine how it must have felt to be burned from pain on the inside as they died. She was at a loss for words for a moment.

"But now you've killed three people," she finally said. "Wouldn't Anna be sad to see what you've become? Is this what she would have wanted?"

Pickles shook his finger at her. "Don't you dare mention my daughter's name! You know nothing about her!"

Zora refused to back down. "Then what about me? I didn't do anything to you, yet you pointed the police in my direction. You'd planned to destroy my life the same way your daughter's life was ruined!" she cried out.

Pickles shook his head vigorously as if trying to drive her voice away. "I did nothing wrong! I'm not going to listen to this nonsense." He picked up a syringe from the bowl near her feet with his gloved hands. It was already filled with clear fluid. "It's all your fault. You had to put your nose into it. And despite my warnings, you wouldn't stop. Now you know too much." He pulled a tourniquet from his pocket and tied it around her arm.

Zora guessed what was about to happen next. She struggled against the restraints. Her heart raced, and sweat broke out on her skin. "Wait! Don't do this!" she cried out.

"Goodbye, Zora." He plunged the needle into the now visible vein in her forearm.

Zora felt a burning sensation begin in her arm and then sweep through her body. Her nerve endings were on fire, and her chest tightened. She screamed and jerked repeatedly against the restraints as her body tried to double over. But the cuffs held her back.

Sorrow filled her heart. For losing her dream, for never seeing Christina and Marcus again, for a lost chance with her mother, and for a life destroyed by revenge and bitterness.

Zora found it harder and harder to breathe. She'd run out of time.

Her vision blurred.

Then everything went pitch black.

34

D rake opened his eyes to see himself naked, shackled with metal restraints to a steel table, a large cleaver knife pointed toward his groin from an overhead anchor. The rotten smell that filled the air made Drake almost throw up.

An enlarged version of a farmhouse sink jutted out from the wall. The room was dank and window-less, and Drake could see large cobwebs and thick layers of dust all over the room. This was a place that hadn't been stepped in for quite a while.

He shivered. Drake wasn't sure how he'd gotten here. He'd taken a drink from Susie the last he'd remembered and had passed out.

Susie. She must have had something to do with

this. He would deal with her later. But first he had to find a way out.

Drake moved his arms and legs to check if the cuffs were secure. Instead, a sharp intense pain pierced his groin, and he arched back on the table. He looked down to see blood pooling on the table from between his legs.

A guttural roar erupted from his throat. Someone had damaged him. He tried to shift his waist slowly, but stabs of pain eclipsed his every move.

He swore. He would get his revenge on the person who'd done this to him. There was only one likely candidate, someone who had the guts to go up against him.

Alfred Pickles.

Well, Drake wouldn't go down easily. He moved his left shoulder. No pain there. That meant the tracking device hadn't been discovered.

He smiled. Once Tiny discovered Drake was missing, he would activate the tracker. And then they would rescue him. All Drake had to do was hold on until then.

Then an unearthly scream echoed from the other side of the wall. Something nasty was going down in the next room.

Drake's heart beat faster, and fear gripped him. *Hurry, Tiny, hurry.*

Soon he grew weaker, and his limbs felt heavier. The pool of blood was now spreading on the table.

Drake shook his head to drive the dizziness away. He didn't know how long he had before he'd pass out.

But he resolved to hang on for as long as he could.

35

Zora struggled to open her eyes, but when she finally succeeded, she found herself lying on what looked like a hospital bed. Low light beamed out from a single light source in the ceiling and cast a warm glow on her. A screen had been drawn around the bed.

Zora turned her head to the right and saw Christina folded into a chair by the side of her bed, her fiery red hair in a ponytail. She looked exhausted and tired.

"Christina?" Zora's voice croaked.

Christina startled awake and looked at Zora's direction. Her eyes widened, and she scrambled forward. "Are you okay?" she said, concern and worry written all over her face. "Thank God you're awake."

Zora tried to move her limbs, but her body felt heavy, tired, and her bones ached. It was like they belonged to someone else.

"Where am I?" Zora asked.

"You are at Lexinbridge Regional Hospital. Everything is okay now." Christina brushed back the hair away from Zora's face.

"How did I—?"

"We found you from the tracker in your pendant. Your mom installed one in it after what happened to your sister."

Zora looked down at the pendant that nestled at the base of her neck. "I didn't know it had a tracking device." She reached up with effort to touch it. It was cool against her fingers. And it had saved her life.

Her mother had saved her life.

An unusual sensation filled her chest. Zora didn't know what it was, but it didn't feel bad. But more immediate questions distracted her.

"How did you guys know to look for me?" she asked.

Christina's green eyes stayed solemn. She sat down on the bed beside Zora. "Remember how I always told you I get super restless whenever I feel something is wrong? I felt that way while at work, and I couldn't concentrate. I finally gave up and got permission to leave early. The ER wasn't that busy, so the other nurse said she could cover for me.

"When I got home, everything seemed normal. That was until I noticed a used blood-tinged syringe and needle discarded on the floor. Once I saw that, I realized something was wrong. The Zora I knew would never be that careless. I checked all the rooms in our apartment and you weren't there.

"Your bag was on the kitchen counter. That was unusual too—I know how you are about your stuff. I searched it and saw the warning note and your phone." Christina cocked her head in mock exasperation. "And you *never* leave your phone behind. So I called Marcus. He knew about the tracking device and called your mom, who activated it. He then called the detectives, told them you'd been kidnapped and who the possible suspect was, and gave them the tracking information. We headed there straightaway and found you in a room in the basement."

"Where?" Zora asked.

"In the Gross Anatomy building on campus. Can you imagine? Right under the same place where the first victim was found." Christina adjusted the sheets around Zora. "The cops searched the other rooms on the floor and found a Drake Pierce lying unconscious next door in a pool of blood around his legs. He was rushed to the hospital, but his genitals were already badly damaged."

"Genitals?"

"Yes. I heard the killer did a number on him. Like a mini-castration."

"Ouch."

"Ouch indeed. I'm not an advocate of violence, but once I heard what he'd done to that poor girl, Anna Hammond, I figured the guy deserved it. No babies in his future except adoption."

"What about Pickles? Did they catch him?"

"Yes, they did. They arrested him as he rushed out of the building. The cops believed someone alerted him that they were on their way, but they haven't found out who."

Zora's shoulders relaxed. She was glad he was no longer a threat.

"You, on the other hand, were lucky," Christina said. "The EMT saw the syringe on the table, suspected what had happened, worked fast on you, and rushed you here. Once you arrived, you were given sodium bicarbonate, lots of fluid, and dialysis to flush the chemicals from your system. Fortunately, no major organs were damaged. I've been here ever since, waiting for you to wake up."

Zora reached for Christina's hand and gave her a warm smile. "Thank you."

Christina placed her other hand on Zora's. "I'm just glad you're okay. It might be a week or two, but the doctors said you'll be back on your feet in no time. Your mom was also here for a while, but she just left for a meeting and said she'd be back once she was done."

It was strange. Zora felt no anger on hearing her mother had left her for a meeting. Maybe a brush with death had changed her.

"Where's Marcus?"

Christina's eyes twinkled. "He refused to leave your side. I literally had to push him to leave. I told him the faster he went with the detectives to the station to give his statement, the faster they could make sure Pickles was locked behind bars. I'm sure he'll come running back here once he's finished. Give me one second." Christina pulled her phone from her pocket and started typing on it.

"What are you doing?"

"I'm sending a text to your mom and Marcus to let them know you're awake."

Zora leaned back further into the pillow and closed her eyes. She couldn't believe it was finally over. She'd almost died and had thought she would never see her friends again.

"Zora?"

Zora opened her eyes. "Yes, I'm here." Seeing the concerning look on Christina's face, she said, "I just needed to close my eyes for a second. I'm not going anywhere."

"You scared me." Zora saw tears had welled up in Christina's eyes. "I thought I had lost you."

Zora reached out for her hand. "I'm fine now."

"Just don't do that to me again."

"I won't," Zora said, patting her hand.

Christina drew in a tremulous breath and tried to smile. "In other news, you're now a celebrity."

"What?"

"It's all over the news. '*Medical student cracks the Formalin Killer case.*' Your phone has been ringing non-stop. Your classmates, the press. I don't know how they got your number. I had to switch it off. Marcus, Silas, and your mom know to call my phone instead."

Zora heard the door open. She swung her head and saw a dark-skinned nurse step in and walk to the foot of the bed.

"How are you doing?" the nurse asked with a smile. "I see you're awake."

"Not too bad," Zora said. "I just feel very tired."

"You should be, after what you've been through. You do need to rest. The doctor will be here shortly." Turning to Christina, she said, "All visitors have to leave now except for family."

"That means I get to stay," a voice said from the door. Marcus stepped in, looking as gorgeous as ever in a grey dress shirt with rolled up sleeves and a pair of jeans. The sling was gone from his left arm. "I'm her fiancé," he said with a deadpan face.

Christina's jaw hung open in shock. A fly could have easily made it in and out of her mouth.

Zora laughed.

"Is it true?" Christina asked Zora in a whisper.

Zora beamed at Marcus. "We'll see," she said with a twinkle in her eye.

Zora looked around the Gross Anatomy lab. It'd been a week since the kidnapping and she'd recovered much faster than everybody had predicted, though she tired easily. The doctors had requested a full body workup just to make sure everything was back to normal, and then she'd been discharged. Marcus had also recovered fully, and Zora was grateful for that.

It felt good to be back. Funny, but she'd missed this place. Maybe because learning to dissect was a big step closer in becoming a surgeon.

The lab had been reopened, and new security measures were already in place to prevent a repeat of what had happened. The rooms in the basement were being renovated into modern autopsy rooms. Thank goodness they would be put to better use.

Pickles had been charged with murder and attempted murder. Silas had mentioned it might not go to trial—Pickles had been diagnosed with end stage interstitial lung disease with about three months to live. He was expected to remain in prison custody until his death. They never did find out who had warned Pickles off.

The detectives had taken Zora's statement in the hospital. Zora had given Detective Morris such a fierce stare throughout the interview that he'd ended up looking away, which gave her a small measure of satisfaction.

A directed search of Professor Oakley's house had revealed the missing rape kit with the forensic results, and Drake Pierce had been charged with the rape of Anna Pickles. There were rumors he'd gone into hiding—no one had reported seeing him since the incident happened. His lawyers were fighting the charge, and Zora was sure they'd run up their bills.

A certain Miss Susie had been found in the river with her throat slit. From her physical appearance, the police had initially thought she was an older version of Zora. Then it turned out she was the mother of Anna Pickles. She'd abandoned Anna when she was only a baby. For some reason, the case had been closed, though the killer had never been found. Zora had a feeling Drake Pierce had a role in that decision.

Danny Thompson was also missing, and the police suspected he might be dead.

But Zora was no longer interested in the case. She was just glad to be alive. It was time to focus back on her life and her work.

Zora looked down at the body on the table. Female, late fifties. She ran a gloved hand over the back. No powder. The professor had re-certified every body in the lab this morning to confirm they were the cadavers they'd requested.

She smiled at her teammates and nodded. It was time to get started.

Zora closed her eyes and bowed her head for a moment of silence for the cadaver. Then she opened her eyes. "Let's begin," she said to her teammates. She took a deep breath and picked up the scalpel.

Her phone rang in her lab coat pocket. Zora had changed her number after the kidnapping, so only a few people had it.

She clenched the scalpel tighter and gave her teammates a forced smile.

But the phone rang again.

"One second," she said and dropped the scalpel in a stainless-steel bowl. She removed her gloves, dropped them in the hazardous waste container under the table, and pulled her phone from her pocket.

"This is Zora Smyth," she said as she walked a few feet away.

"Miss Smyth, this is Dr. Wang." Dr. Wang was her primary care physician and had been for several years.

"Hi, Dr. Wang. What's going on?"

"Would it be possible for you to come by my office tomorrow? Afternoon would be best."

"What is it? Is something wrong? Just give it to me straight."

"Are you in an appropriate place to talk?"

Zora strode toward the door and exited the lab. There was no one in the hallway. "Yes, I can talk now."

"Your CBC results just came in. Your neutrophil and WBC counts are abnormally low, and we found some blast cells as well. We'd like you to come in and get a confirmatory bone marrow aspiration and biopsy done."

Zora's breath hitched, and her heart raced. "What do you think is wrong?" she said. "You can tell me."

"The results so far are indicative of Acute Lymphocytic Leukemia."

There was a brief pause on the line.

"Zora, we think you might have cancer."

Thank you so much for reading!

Want to know what happens next to Dr. Zora Smyth? You can grab LETHAL INCISION at https://dobicross.com

If you've loved reading LETHAL DISSECTION, Dobi would be grateful if you could spend a few minutes to leave a review (as short as you like) on the book's page on your favorite retailer. Your review would help bring it to the attention of other readers. Thank you very much.

Check out all Dobi Cross books at https://dobicross.com

ACKNOWLEDGMENTS

Writing a book is harder and more rewarding than I could have ever imagined. And it would not have been possible without the support, love, and encouragement from my number one cheerleader, my dearest mom. My life would never have been this awesome and wonderful without you.

Of course, I have to thank my precious little DC for his smiles and antics. You brighten my day and give me the strength to keep pushing through.

Thank you to my sisters for encouraging me on this wonderful journey. And a special thanks to my baby brother (who is so not a baby anymore) for being super supportive and checking in on my progress. You guys are the best.

Thank you to my wonderful author friends. You know who you are. Your selflessness and willingness to share what you know has made my writing journey smoother and an exciting one. And a special thanks to Lisa and Deanna whose support have made a difference.

Most of all, I want to thank God who gave me life, surrounded me with the most wonderful people, and loved me all the way. You make my life complete.

And finally, a special thanks to all my readers whose love of my stories spur me on to write more. Thank you!

ABOUT THE AUTHOR

As a former physician and business executive in another life—with a childhood filled with reading multi-genre novels (including Shakespeare in the original version)—Dobi Cross loves to write thrilling stories with heart.

She enjoys dreaming up everyday characters who rise above unfavorable circumstances to overcome incredible odds. When not writing, Dobi can be found binging K-dramas and ice cream with her little sidekick by her side.

Lethal Dissection is the first book in the Zora Smyth Medical Thriller Series. Sign up at https://dobi-cross.com to be notified when the next Dobi Cross book comes out!

Thanks for reading LETHAL DISSECTION!